Trusted

- books in the -
Dragons' Trust Series

Trusted
Burned
Stolen
Tempered

Trusted

Dragons' Trust Book 1

Krista Wayment

Trusted

By Krista Wayment

First Edition, March 2014

Copyright © 2014 Krista Wayment

Cover Art Title copyright © 2014 Krista Wayment

Cover Art Dragon copyright © DM7 (Shutterstock)

Cover Art Background copyright © LilKar (Shutterstock)

Illustrations copyright © 2014 Krista Wayment

ISBN: 1495482294
ISBN-13: 978-1495482298

For my children.
You are my all, my everything.

Prologue

A thousand years ago, our kind made a fatal mistake. We reached out to the young race of man to offer our guidance. We shared our knowledge and wisdom of the earth, healing, metal work, and many other things. At first, all was well. Man and dragon lived in peace, working side by side for the benefit of all.

This delicate balance shifted when man gave in to their greatest failing—greed. Then what we had shared with them was turned against us.

Men sought a most rare and precious treasure: the heart stones of dragons. They granted unbelievable power and unnaturally long life to the possessor. The hunting began. We dragons were hunted down—some were killed, others captured. Our numbers diminished at an alarming rate and man started to breed us like common cattle.

They thought they could harvest the stone from our young. They were wrong. In order to thwart their efforts to subvert our race, our ancestors withheld the Awakening from the next generation of dragons.

A new kind of dragon was born. These new dragons were mute and devoid of intelligence, but most importantly, their heart stones were dim and empty. Our mute brothers and sisters are now enslaved, forced to labor and serve the very kind who robbed them of their greatness.

Those who remain of the old dragons live as fugitives, hiding from the ever-growing reach of man. We are fading from the world, disappearing into the darkness of history. But we will not go quietly. We intend to fight.

Flyer

The dragon's call ripped through the crisp morning air. Renick looked up to watch the dragon approach. A beautiful red winged her way toward the landing area. Her melodious trumpeting seemed to echo and fade across the treetops. According to legend, her song was composed of her name and pedigree, and embodied who she was as a dragon. Renick wondered, if the legend were true, what such a song would really sound like.

Spreading her wings wide, the dragon let her tail fall and hovered high above his head. The tow lines that were harnessed to the magnificent beast slackened. The handler, who perched on a board suspended in the tow lines, stood and wrapped his arm around one of the ropes. A passenger basket, made from woven reeds, came into view as it sank below the dragon. Renick could see the kiter in the basket working the rigging to hold the kite steady. One of the canvas sails folded under the command of the kiter and the basket dipped a little closer to the grassy ground.

Dane ruffled Renick's already disheveled brown hair. "Nervous, Rub?"

Renick shrugged, an action that brought an amused smile to his older brother's face.

3

"Uncle Loren won't bite, but some of the dragons he stables might." Dane winked at him and then elbowed Jon, his next older brother.

"Yeah, just come back from your apprenticeship with all your fingers, else you won't be any use to us." Jon punched Renick's shoulder.

"You two leave him alone." Renick's mother, Anngene, placed her hands on her hips and with a scolding look on her face added, "And go round up the little ones. We need to get heading back as soon as we see Renick off."

Dane and Jon took turns rubbing their fists into Renick's head before they scampered off to herd the younger children back to their mother. They chased after Mandy and Josie. Over and over again, the two girls deftly escaped their brothers' hold. Chasing them would never work. You had to coax Mandy and Josie into a trap, but Dane and Jon would never think of that. All the while, little baby Angie sat in the middle of the grass wailing, a crushed daisy clutched in her small hands.

Despite the chaos, Renick's mother turned a soft smile on him. "Don't you listen to them. Everything will be fine. Your father will come check on you in a couple of months. Four years will go by before you know it." Her eyes filled with tears, and a little catch cut off the last of her words. She hugged Renick to her large form and kissed his forehead. "Take care," his mother whispered. Lifting her head, she yelled, "Mandy! Get down from there." Releasing her hold on her youngest son, his mother marched off to rescue his failing brothers.

Standing alone watching the usual family antics, Renick felt a growing anxiety that threatened to steal his lunch as well as his ability to breathe. He would be on his own for the first time in his life. Renick closed his eyes and recited the list of reasons why getting away from his large family would be exciting. He made it halfway through when the tension in his stomach eased. Renick let out a sigh of relief. Losing his last meal in front of his brothers would unleash a maelstrom of taunts and ridicule.

There was a soft *whoosh* as the passenger basket of the flyer settled on the grass. Renick turned to watch the graceful descent of the dragon, the wind from her beating wings pushing against him. The travelers disembarked while the men from the landing area unloaded their belongings from compartments that also served as benches. The kiter busied himself with inspecting the sails, his fingers running over each seam and edge. Meanwhile, the handler saw to his dragon, ensuring that she was properly fed and watered before the next excursion.

A scream drew Renick's attention away from the scene and back to the pandemonium that was his family. Mandy had climbed up the watchtower and was skipping happily around it. The watchmen yelled for her to get down, but their words were swallowed by a shrill order to behave from Renick's mother. Renick sighed and started to walk toward them.

"All aboard!" a voice called.

Renick stopped. The other four passengers who had been waiting—a healer woman, a young girl, a boy just older than himself, and an old knight—were climbing into the flyer. Renick did not know what to do. He stood debating between boarding and assisting his mother. If he got in the passenger basket now, he would not get to say good-bye to his family. On the other hand, if he waited too long, the flyer would leave without him.

"Last call, all aboard!" The man looked pointedly at Renick.

A jumble of arms and faces surrounded Renick, squeezing him tightly.

"Bye!"

"We'll miss you—"

"Have fun—"

"Good luck—"

they all seemed to say together.

And then they released him and he was ushered into the basket. Renick watched as his mother took a firm grip on Mandy and Josie, ordered Dane to scoop up the baby, and led her family back to the wagon. Renick sat in the front, partially turned so he could lean his chin on the railing and watch the dragon during takeoff.

"Ho!" the handler, who stood between the dragon and the passenger basket, called.

"Ho hep!" came the reply from the kiter, who was already positioned in the basket just a few paces from where Renick sat.

In response to a pull on the reins from the handler, the dragon raised her wings and began to beat them backwards. The men from the landing area picked up the kite and held the giant canvas up into the path of the wind created by the dragon. The kite rose into the air until it caught a current of air and pulled taut. The dragon changed the angle of her wings and started to lift her body into the air. As the tow lines followed her, the handler's perch righted itself and he stepped up onto it. The last to leave the ground was the passenger basket. Once all the components of the flyer were airborne, the dragon began moving forward, towing the basket and the kite behind her.

Before long, the dragon was flying gracefully above the forest canopy, pulling the passenger basket and kite behind it. Renick's eyes traced the methodical beat of the dragon's almost translucent wings. A small gasp broke the stillness. Renick looked up to see the blond girl traveling with the healer woman standing near him.

"She's beautiful," the girl said with awe. "I wonder what kind she is." The girl leaned far over the basket, her head tilted to the side so she could see the dragon. She smiled and wiggled her head, which made her hair dance in the wind.

Worried that she might fall to a horrible death, Renick relinquished his silence. "She's a mountain red. They're the best fliers, and have the most brilliant colors."

To Renick's relief, the girl leaned back to a safer perch.

"What's your name?" she asked, her gray eyes boring into him.

"Renick."

"I'm Lainey." She thrust out her hand. Renick reluctantly

took it, noticing that the other passengers were watching them. Understandable, since they seemed to be the only two talking.

"So ..." Lainey leaned forward, bracing herself against the edge of the basket with her folded arms and pulling her knees up onto the bench. "How did you know what kind of dragon she is? And that it is a 'she,' for that matter?" Lainey smiled at him as she waited for a response.

Renick cleared his throat. "My father is a dragon breeder." He pointed to the dragon. "See how the horns curl at the ends? That's how you can tell she's a mountain breed. And she doesn't have a thagomizer at the end her tail, so it's a she. At least that's true for mountain breeds."

"Ah. You know a lot about dragons." After a quick glance over her shoulder, Lainey turned back to him. "My aunt's a healer. She works mostly with people, but she does a lot of dragon stuff, too."

Renick looked at the older woman sitting on a bench behind the kiter. Her dark hair was pulled back in a tight bun, and her thin lips were drawn together. She seemed very sober in both dress and demeanor. Very unlike her niece.

"... anyway, so that's why we are traveling to Trevinni. I'm going to train with her to be a healer."

Renick blinked and looked up, unsure how he could have missed that Lainey was still talking. Lainey turned around in a circle, the skirt of her patched blue dress fanning out around her, and sat next to him.

"What do you think of that boy over there?" she asked.

He turned his attention to the two remaining passengers. The boy Lainey spoke of was obviously highborn. The pristine fabric of his clothes bore the symbols of a noble house. An ornate sword was strapped around his waist. The man sitting next to him, with a stern expression on his face, wore the garb of a soldier. The soldier's hair was graying and deep lines defined his face, but his eyes were bright and alert.

The boy tossed his black hair and looked toward Lainey, the corner of his mouth twitching just a little. Renick turned back to Lainey and saw an expectant expression on her face.

He could only shrug in reply.

"Well, he didn't seem very talkative to me. I think he might be a snob. Just making polite conversation, I was. My aunt tells me that I talk too much which can be off-putting. It's not like I don't give others a chance to say things. I just don't like silence, so I fill it up. Don't you think having polite conversation with someone is better than just sitting here in silence?"

Renick realized she was waiting for him to respond again. He blinked a couple of times before he spoke. "I don't know. I think I like them both the same."

"Ah." Lainey bit her lower lip and swung her feet a few times. "Well, I think talking is better. He may be cute, but I really think it was rude of him not to talk to me. At least a hello or something. A small exchange of pleasantries. Really, I should've expected as much. You know, from his sort." She rolled her eyes and flicked her hand as if she was annoyed. "Do you think I talk too much?"

This time Renick did not have time to form a proper response. All he managed to get out was, "Well …"

"Of course you don't. I can tell. You are the sort of boy who would've told me by now if you did. But really, I don't think you are capable of thinking so." She smiled warmly at Renick and stole a glance at the other boy. "How old are you?"

"Uh, fourteen."

"Really? You look older than that. Like you could be that boy's age." She leaned on her hands and tossed her head in the highborn's direction. Renick thought he did not look that much older. He was probably only fifteen or sixteen.

"I am only twelve," Lainey continued. "But my aunt says I can start an apprenticeship early on account of me being an orphan …" She trailed off, dipping her head as if ashamed.

A strange whistling noise tickled Renick's ears. His eyes scanned the sky and the forest below in search of its sound. He saw Lainey's aunt frantically waving a hand in her direction, trying to get her attention. The stern-faced man looked around with narrowed eyes. The other boy sat with his arms crossed, his brown eyes trained on Lainey, who had turned back to

Renick, her mouth open to speak.

And then the world seemed to slow down.

Something—a long, dark something—cut through the bright-blue sky heading straight for them from the depths of the forest below. Renick watched, stunned, as the dark spot tore its way through the tight fabric of the sails. The sound of separating fibers sent a chill down his spine.

The passenger basket bounced. The kiter leapt into action, attempting to control the darting sails as best he could. He may have shouted something to the handler below, but Renick could not hear it over the agonized wails of the dragon.

Renick turned and looked over the edge of the basket to see the beautiful red thrashing in pain, her wings becoming helplessly tangled in her harness and tow lines. Renick felt a twinge of sadness. In midair, there was no way to free her from the leather straps, and with her wings bound, she could not fly. He knew what was coming. If they stayed connected to the dragon, she would pull them to the ground with her. A flash of light reflected off the handler's blade as he cut at the harness ropes. The last thread holding the flyer to the dragon fell away and the passenger basket swayed slightly. The dragon spiraled downward and crashed into the forest. Free of the twisting, heavy burden, the erratic descent of the basket slowed. The handler pressed his fingers to his lips briefly, biding the dragon farewell. He turned and started to climb up the now-loose ropes toward the basket.

Renick heard a tearing sound and looked up in time to see the main sail divide itself in half.

The breath rushed out of his lungs and his stomach leapt into his throat.

They were falling.

Falling

The Forest

Renick's shoulder hurt. He tried to move his arm, but it did not respond. He urged his eyes to open and begged his voice to call for help. Nothing. The smell of soil filled his nose as he took a deep breath. After a second breath, Renick was finally able to force his eyes open.

Green. All he could see was green. A breeze jostled the leaves and a few drops of sunlight filtered through the branches. Renick shot up to a sitting position. Pain pierced his right arm and he cried out. When his vision cleared, Renick realized he was on the wrong side of the forest canopy. He should not be on the ground.

The sensation of falling came rushing back to him, but nothing else. He must have been knocked out during the crash.

Renick moved to stand, which caused a burning pain to radiate through his shoulder. He turned to look at it and saw that something bulged unnaturally. He tried to stand again, this time supporting his injured arm with his left hand. It took some inventive footwork, but Renick managed to climb to his feet. He leaned against a tree for a moment, waiting for the pain to subside so he could move again.

The passenger basket lay on the ground. It had tipped over onto its side and stood wedged between two large tree trunks.

The sails, or what remained of them, were tangled in the trees above. There was no sign of the kiter, the handler, or any of the other passengers.

"Hello?" Renick called. "Hello!"

A faint moan emanated from the shadowy depths of the passenger basket. Renick picked his way over to it and poked his head in. Blond hair spilled over the woven sides of the craft.

"Lainey?" The pain in Renick's shoulder prevented him from climbing over the debris to get closer. "Lainey."

She moaned again. The hair shifted and her nose appeared. "Lainey!"

She turned her head to look at him. "What're you doing up there, Renick?" She asked in a sleepy voice.

"The flyer crashed. We're on the forest floor. You need to wake up."

With slow, unsteady movements, Lainey managed to get herself into a sitting position. She stared at him with glassy eyes. "Crashed?" She blinked a few times and looked around her. As she took in her surroundings, the fog cleared from her eyes and was replaced by something else. Renick thought it might be fear. "Where's everyone?" The words came out even and slow, but Lainey's hands were shaking.

"I don't know. Let's go look for them."

Lainey started to climb down from the overturned basket. Renick offered her his hand. She took it, gripping more firmly than necessary. When both her feet rested firmly on the ground, she turned to look at him.

"It's dislocated," she said.

"What?"

"Your shoulder." She pointed to his injured arm. "It's dislocated. Lie down over here." Lainey pointed to a place near one of the larger trees. She helped Renick lower himself to the ground and sat next to him. She placed one foot against the tree and one in the pit of his injured arm. Renick winced. "Sorry, this is going to hurt pretty badly. But I promise it will be better in the long run." Grasping his wrist with both of her hands, Lainey leaned back and pulled gently on the injured arm. Renick clenched his jaw, squeezed his eyes shut, and concentrated on not screaming.

Something popped in his shoulder. The brief flash of pain caught Renick off guard and a small shriek escaped. The pressure of Lainey's fingers evaporated from his wrist.

"Renick, I need you to open your eyes and look at me," she said, her voice heavy with concern. He opened his eyes and found her face. Lainey studied him. "Good, I can see the blue in your eyes, which means you aren't in shock. Your shoulder will be sore for a while and may never be the same again," she explained as she helped Renick back to his feet. "I would fashion you a sling, but ..." her eyes circled the wreckage, "it may be more of a hindrance right now."

He rolled his shoulder and experimented with its movement. The muscles were stiff and sore, but he could manage well enough. "Thanks."

Lainey's lips turned upward, but that something still haunted her eyes. "Healer's niece." She pointed to herself. "Handy to have in a situation like this."

Renick managed a small laugh and Lainey gave him another half smile in return.

The bushes to Renick's left rustled and a growl lifted from their depths. Lainey gasped and ducked behind Renick, burying her face between his shoulder blades. Renick froze. Neither his arms nor his legs would respond to any commands.

A head covered in dark hair emerged from the bushes. Renick's breath came out in a rush. The highborn boy turned to glare at them. His face was covered in bruises and small scratches.

"Oh!" Lainey exclaimed. The boy's eyes narrowed and he continued to struggle against the branches and leaves. Lainey started to giggle. The boy set his mouth in a grim line and focused on Renick.

Renick moved to help, pulling at the branches. The other boy finally tumbled free of the vengeful plant and onto the ground. Renick picked at a fresh tear in his muslin shirt. It was the new one his mother had made for him to celebrate his apprenticeship. She would be horrified to see it in the state it was. At least his brown leather pants were faring better.

The boy pushed himself off the ground and back to his feet. Fishing in the bushes, he pulled out his sword and fastened the belt into its proper place.

"I'm Lainey." She stepped up to them and extended her hand to the newcomer. Her hand hung in the air, waiting. The boy did not look at her. Instead, he busied himself with brushing off his clothes. Renick shifted his feet—it was not appropriate for Lainey to address a nobleman that way.

Renick cleared his throat. "I am Renick Banguebar, apprentice dragonhand." He bent himself in half in a respectful bow. "This is Lainey ..."

The smile that had been frozen on Lainey's face fell away. She turned and stormed off into the wreckage of the basket. The boy watched after her for a moment.

Renick cleared his throat again.

"Sir Thane Shaytorrin, son of Lord Shay of the Westfields," the boy introduced himself.

Renick bowed again. "Milord."

Thane's shoulders dropped. "Look," he said, "given the situation, I think we can dispense with the pleasantries." Thane blew a puff of air at the hair hanging in his face and held out his hand. "I'm Thane."

Renick felt a little uncomfortable shaking Thane's hand, but he did not want to offend.

"So, any signs of the others?" Thane asked as he looked around the small clearing.

"No, but then again, we haven't really searched."

Thane looked up at the sky. "It will be dark soon. We will make the best camp we can here. At first light, we will begin the search."

"Aunt Melatheen," Lainey called into the forest around them.

Thane shushed her. "Didn't you hear what I just said? We'll search in the morning!"

"Who said you were in charge?" Lainey said, poking her head around the back of the passenger basket. Lainey and Thane exchanged glares. Lainey won by sticking out her tongue, which made Thane's mouth twitch.

Lainey took a deep breath. "Aunt Melatheen!" This time she was even louder.

A low grumble echoed through the trees. Lainey jumped a little and back-stepped closer to where Renick and Thane were standing.

Folding his arms, Thane looked at her. "Do you want to attract every meat-eating monster in the forest?"

"We have to look for them." Lainey's voice was almost pleading. "Renick, what do you think?"

He cast a nervous glance over at Thane before responding. "Uh, it's not my place ..."

"What do you think?" Lainey said, marching to stand next to him. She put her small, pointed nose right up to his rounder one; she had to stand on her tiptoes to reach.

"Well, since we're lost and separated from the others, the best thing would be to stay put. So," he looked up at Thane again, who stood with his arms crossed and his lips pursed, "we should make camp."

Lainey's stern expression broke out into a smile. "What an excellent idea." She spun on her heels and started hunting around, humming to herself as she went. "I'll get some firewood."

Renick watched her for a moment before turning to face Thane. Thane's brow was furrowed, his fists on his hips as he watched Lainey's movements.

"All right then," Renick said to himself.

"We should scavenge in the wreckage—there could be any number of useful things," Thane said. He waved his hand about. Renick nodded his head and started walking around the area where the trees were a little thinner than the rest of the forest. Thane searched too, but Renick noticed he stayed clear of Lainey. Renick wondered why—Lainey was not that bad.

By the time the sunlight was fading, Thane and Renick had

recovered two emergency rucksacks that contained waterskins and dried food as well as a large piece of sail they could use for shelter. Lainey had found her traveling pack, her healer's pouch, and three travelling cloaks. Renick filled the waterskins in a stream he found nearby.

Using flint and steel Thane found in one of the packs, he soon had a modest fire going. The three of them sat around the flames, chewing on bits of dried meat and fruit.

Lainey sighed. "What happened?"

Renick shrugged.

"I think we were shot down," Thane speculated. "I didn't get a good look at ... whatever it was, but it had to be a weapon of some kind. What else could injure a dragon and split the sails?"

Renick cocked his head to one side. "Who would want to shoot us down?"

"Could it have been bandits?" Lainey asked. Her eyes grew big and she turned her head to look at the trees behind her.

Thane shook his head. "I don't know. But for now I think it best we keep an eye out. We'll need to set a watch. I'll go first."

Up a Tree

Renick woke to the sound of Lainey's scream piercing the night. In the dying light of the fire, he saw Thane's silhouette standing with sword drawn, facing the darkness. Six pairs of glowing eyes stared back at them.

A series of low rumbles rolled out from the space beyond the circle of firelight. Jaws filled with gleaming fangs snapped together.

"Wolves," Renick whispered.

Lainey whimpered and pulled her knees up to her chest. She started rocking back and forth, mumbling something under her breath.

"Renick," Thane said in an even tone, "do you have a weapon?"

"No."

"Find one."

Renick moved slowly around inside the wrecked basket, his hands feeling in the dark for anything. His fingers found a beam of wood that had been broken off from a bench. He took hold of it and stood. "Got it."

A wolf lunged at Thane. Lainey screamed. Thane swung his blade, reflections of yellow light dancing along the metal. A yelp rang through the clearing. The wolf withdrew. When

Thane brought his sword back to the ready position, Renick noticed a dark stain running down it. Somewhere out in the darkness, the sounds of the wolf's death throes reverberated through the night.

Two wolves emerged from the darkness. Thane brought his blade down on the first one. Renick ran into the fray, swinging the beam at the second wolf. The animal caught the wood in its powerful jaws and thrashed its head back and forth. Renick tightened his grip and kicked at the beast. From the far corner of the basket, Renick could hear Lainey crying. The wolf pulled Renick's piece of wood to the ground. Seizing the opportunity, Renick drove his foot down on the beast's head. The opposing hold on the wood vanished as the wolf retreated.

Renick chanced a quick look at Thane. They had both moved forward about two paces and were now further apart with their backs exposed. Blood coated Thane's sword. With his opponent no longer in sight, Thane took the time to clean his sword on the grass.

"Up a tree," Thane said. "We need to get up a tree."

The wolves started to close in again. Renick looked back to see that Lainey had not moved. "Thane," Renick called, "Lainey needs help."

"I need a diversion," Thane said as he swung his blade in a wide arch. The wolves paused, but continued to move forward.

Renick's eyes darted around the shrinking area between where they stood and the enemy. His attention was caught by the slight flickering of the fire. "All right, on the count of three, you go help Lainey." Out of the corner of his eye, Renick saw Thane nod. "One, two, three."

Jumping forward, Renick swept his stick across the remains of the fire, scattering it. Half a dozen large embers spread through the air directly at the wolves. One of the embers, its flame brought to life by the increase in air, landed on the back of one of the animals. The wolf whined in fear, running in circles in an attempt to flee the growing flame. It disappeared into the thick trees of the forest. The other embers lit the dry grass, creating an uneven line of fire that held the wolves at bay. Renick started to back up, keeping his eyes trained on the four remaining attackers. Soon he was standing next to Thane and Lainey near the edge of the passenger basket. Thane had coaxed Lainey to stand up and follow him. She cowered behind him as he held his blade out in the direction of the wolf pack. Thane tilted his head toward one of the trees that the basket was wedged between.

Renick threw his makeshift weapon at one of the wolves, who skirted away from it. Turning, he bounded up the tree as quickly as his sore shoulder would allow. When he reached the first sturdy branch, he stopped and reached down with his good arm. Thane sheathed his sword and lifted Lainey until she could reach Renick's outstretched fingers. Renick provided an anchor and leverage to Lainey as she climbed up the tree. Thane followed closely behind her.

Down on the forest floor, the wolves howled and snapped their jaws at the waning flames. Slowly the light from the shattered fire dissipated and the wolves closed in. They scratched at the bark of the tree and tried to jump up it. Eventually, one of the wolves abandoned the tree and managed to get on top of the passenger basket. One good leap and the wolf would be upon them.

Thane, who was the closest to the wolf, reached down to his boot and drew out a knife. He held it ready as he watched the wolf's movements. The gray animal growled, its sharp teeth bared and menacing.

A thundering roar rolled through the air, echoing across the entire forest. Renick clapped his hands over his ears to stave off some of the volume. He turned to look at the wolf. It had stopped advancing toward them. Its ears were laid back and its tail hung down between its legs. The other three wolves on the ground were behaving in the same manner. They milled around the wolf Thane had killed with his sword. Another roar sent the small pack scurrying into the depths of the forest.

"What was that?" Lainey said, her voice shaking.

"Sounds like a dragon," Renick answered.

"No dragon I've ever heard," Thane said.

"Probably a wild one. I've heard—" Renick was interrupted by a loud crash and the sound of many branches breaking at once.

All was silent.

After a long while, Lainey chanced a whispered question. "Is it coming after us?"

Thane shook his head. "I think if it was, we would have seen or heard it by now."

"That did *not* sound like a graceful landing," Renick commented. "I think it may have been injured."

"Like our dragon?" Lainey asked.

Renick just shrugged, an awkward movement when balancing on a tree branch.

"Two dragons being shot down in one day?" Thane said. "That can't be a coincidence."

"What's out there?" Lainey asked.

Renick did not have a good answer for her. There was a reason no one ever traveled by foot through the Helath Forest—wolves, bears, wild dragons, and every kind of frightening beast roamed between the trees. From end to end at its narrowest point, the forest would take a month to cross on foot. Renick closed his eyes and tried to remember where they had been when the flyer went down. Once he had the picture of those last moments in his mind, he studied it carefully. They had not been that far from the edge of the forest. He remembered seeing the open plains on the horizon.

"That's it, then," Renick said aloud.

"What?" Thane asked.

Renick's cheeks started to feel warm as they colored with embarrassment. He cleared his throat and tried to make it seem as if he had not been talking to himself. "We can't stay here."

Lainey and Thane stared at him open-mouthed. "You can't seriously be suggesting that we venture deeper into the forest," Thane said.

"What about the others?" Lainey asked.

"It's too dangerous to search for them. Besides, they might be ..." Renick trailed off and glanced in Lainey's direction when she caught her breath.

"We're lost, Renick," Thane said, his voice deep and cold. "If we stay put, we have the best chance of being found."

"*If* we're found," Renick said.

Lainey let out a short sob.

"We will be found. We stay here," Thane commanded.

Renick shifted his position on the branch. Thane was older and higher in station, and it was not Renick's place to question his judgment. But he could not help it; he knew it was not safe. "But—"

"We stay."

The force in Thane's words ended the debate. Renick started picking at a piece of loose bark on the branch in front of him. He stared at it long after the light from the fire faded and left them in darkness.

Staying was not safe. The dead wolf would attract other predators and scavengers. Not to mention, the wolves would most likely return to mark their territory. He let his hand fall away from the tree branch. He quickly counted in his mind. Five. It would take a rescue party from Trevinni at least five days to reach them.

A painful emptiness rolled through Renick's stomach. "And what about food?"

"What was that?" Thane's voice sliced through the darkness.

"Nothing." Renick hung his head and felt in the dark for his loose piece of bark. He wanted to push for leaving. Could he strike out on his own? No, staying together presented their best chance for survival.

"I'm hungry too." Lainey's voice sounded harsh and spent.

"We will eat in the morning," Thane told her.

The world grew a little lighter as the sun started to rise. A vengeful howl broke through the stillness. The sound of animals moving through the trees approached them. Their scampering feet circled the tree twice and then disappeared into the forest.

"I think it would be unsafe to remain here," Thane said, as

if he had just thought of it. "I think we should strike out and try to find our way to Trevinni." He cleared his throat and looked off into the distance.

In the growing light of morning, Renick turned to look at Lainey. She caught his gaze and rolled her eyes in an exaggerated movement. Another howl, more distant this time, sent a chill up Renick's spine. He turned to watch the sun rise, grateful it was morning.

Broken Wing

Renick slid down the tree and landed with a slight thud next to Thane. The small area around the passenger basket was now filled with light. As Lainey descended from the tree, she lost her balance and fell to the ground. With a sigh, Thane reached down and offered Lainey his hand. She ignored it, but when Renick reached to help her stand, she accepted.

"Thanks, Renick," she said, flashing him a smile.

"We ready?" Thane asked. When Renick turned to look at him, Thane had his arms crossed over his chest and one of the packs on his back.

"What about breakfast?" Lainey asked.

"We can eat while we walk," Thane told her. He held out a chunk of dried bread to both of them.

Renick took his portion of food and picked up the second pack from where it sat on the ground next to Thane's feet. Lainey slung her healer's pouch over her shoulder before taking her piece of bread from Thane's outstretched hand.

"Right. Stay close." Without waiting for a response, Thane marched into the forest. Lainey looked at Renick and rolled her eyes. He could only shrug in response and then follow after Thane.

The forest was cool and quiet in the late morning. The

ground was a mottled combination of light and shadow that shifted back and forth in the breeze. Renick was struck by how loud their passage was in the silence. Not even birds could be heard flitting between the trees. The stillness was almost eerie. A small, thin cry caught Renick's attention. He recognized the sound from many nights spent in the brooder during hatching season. A baby dragon. He stopped and cocked his head.

The cry came again.

Turning from the trail, Renick headed toward the source of the noise. Every time the high-pitched plea sounded through the dense trees, he adjusted his direction. He stepped between two giant trunks and the forest ended abruptly. A deep gouge, some fifty paces wide and about waist deep, ran through the trees and underbrush. Renick looked up and down the pocket of destruction. The motionless tail of a gray dragon snaked out from under a pile of unearthed trees and brush. Renick climbed over the debris until he stood over the tail. Reaching down, he ran his hand over the silvery scales. They were cold.

"Oh," Lainey gasped. Renick turned. Lainey stood behind him, her mouth covered and her eyes surveying the damage. "Was it our dragon?" Her eyes brimmed with tears.

Renick stood. "No, this is a wild dragon. Probably the one we heard last night." He pointed down at the tail. "See, she was a gray."

"She? But she has a thag-a-ma-jig," Lainey said.

"With wild dragons, both genders can have them," Renick said.

"Then how—" Lainey started to say.

"—expected to keep you alive when you wander off!" Thane burst into the clearing. With hardly a glance at the area around him or a pause to breathe, he continued with his ranting. "It's dangerous. Don't you two get that?"

"Shh." Renick thought he heard the cry again. When Thane did not stop talking, Renick shushed him again and closed his eyes to hear better.

This time the cry was clear and very close. Renick picked his way through the wake of ruined ground until he found a small mound of slate-blue scales and black spikes. The mound shifted and a small angular head emerged. The baby dragon, which was roughly the size of a small lamb, flared its nostrils and moaned. Renick crouched down on one knee. He held out his hand, limp at the wrist, and clicked his tongue softly.

The dragon blinked its black eyes at Renick, turning its head from side to side. It cried plaintively and moved with an awkward tilt. Without touching it, Renick carefully inspected the baby dragon's limbs. He also watched for signs of fear or anger from the little predator.

"Aw." Lainey fell to her knees next to Renick. Before he could stop her, she reached out and started stroking the baby dragon's head. To his astonishment, the dragon started to vibrate, much like a silent purr.

"Be careful, Lainey. He's wild and injured. He could turn on you at any moment," Renick said.

"Don't worry." Lainey sounded like Renick's mom when she talked to his baby sister. "It won't hurt us."

Renick continued with his evaluation of the dragon. The radius bone just below the elbow on the left wing was bent at an odd angle; the area around it was swollen and bloody. "His wing is broken."

"The poor thing." Lainey cupped the dragon's head in her hands. "Let's see if we can patch you up."

"Leave it," Thane said coldly.

Renick looked up to find Thane towering over them. "It will slow us down," he offered by way of an argument.

Next to him, Lainey snorted.

"And eat most of our food," Thane tried again.

Renick turned back to the dragon. "He's young enough that he won't need much."

"And its mother will come after us."

"Its mother is dead," Lainey blurted. She looked over at Renick, her eyes sad. "He needs us."

"No," Thane said.

Renick stood and spun around to face Thane. "Who put you in charge?" he demanded. Before the words finished leaving his mouth, he started to lose his nerve. Thane looked so intimidating, especially with his hand on the pommel of his sword like that. Renick felt a reassuring hand touch the back of his leg. "This dragon is hurt, and we can help it. Right?" Renick turned to Lainey who stood up next to him.

"Right." She crossed her arms. With a sideways glance at Renick, she added, "You don't scare us," and stuck out her tongue. Thane just stared back at her, his mouth pressed in a tight line.

"All right, then." Renick knelt back down next to the dragon. Lainey joined him. She pulled her shoulder bag around to the front and opened it.

"I know how to treat human broken bones, but not dragon ones," she said, riffling through the contents of her bag. "Are they similar?"

Renick nodded. "These are. Some of the bones in the wings are hollow, but here where it's broken, they aren't. So the basics should be the same."

"Okay." Lainey spread her hands out over the dragon. "Step one—clean the wound."

Renick picked up the dragon and positioned it on his lap. He wrapped his left arm around the dragon's neck and held the injured wing out to Lainey with his other hand.

"You've handled baby dragons before," Lainey commented.

Renick shrugged. "I helped in my father's brooder a lot."

Lainey smiled at him. Behind them, Thane grumbled and stalked off.

Using a small knife, Lainey cut a strip of bandage from a long roll and used her waterskin to wet it. She pulled a small bottle from her pouch and sprinkled a little of the contents on the bandage. "This is going to sting," she warned. With gentle hands, she cleaned the wound around the broken bone.

The baby dragon resisted and cried out, but Renick held him well enough for Lainey to finish her work. Renick suddenly had an idea. "Wait here," he told Lainey, handing her the dragon.

Renick went over to the pile of trees from which the gray

dragon's tail emanated. He saw Thane dart behind a tree as he approached, but decided to think nothing of it. He started to dig through the dirt and branches until he found the side of the dead dragon. Working away from the tail, Renick continued to dig. At length he found the head. Reaching down, he pried the once-powerful jaws open and reached inside. When he withdrew his hand, his fingers were covered in a clear sticky substance—the dragon's spit.

"Perfect," he said to himself. He returned to where Lainey and the dragon waited.

"What's that?" Lainey asked.

"His mother's saliva. My father says it has healing properties. There are old stories that talk about when dragons used to be able to heal men. But they are either false or it no longer works. This should help the little guy, though."

Lainey nodded. "Good idea."

Renick took the baby dragon back into his lap and smeared the spit on its broken wing. "There. Now what's next?"

"Step two—set the bone." Lainey looked up at Renick, her brow creased. "But if I don't know how the bone is supposed to be, I might set it wrong."

"Try feeling the other wing," Renick said.

Lainey did. "Okay, I think I can do it. Be ready—this will hurt the little guy."

Renick nodded and tightened his hold on the baby dragon.

"On three." Lainey took the wing in both hands. "One ... two ... three."

She pulled. The bone snapped into place. The dragon flinched. A piercing wail rang out. Renick whispered in the baby dragon's ear to sooth it while Lainey inspected her work.

"There. Step three—splint and bandage." She looked around. "We'll need something for a splint."

A pair of equally sized branches stripped of their bark appeared next to Renick's head. Renick turned. Thane held out the perfectly made splints, but he was looking off in the other direction.

Lainey took the pieces of wood. "Thank you," she said.

Thane just turned away.

Lainey held the splints in her hands for a few moments and then turned back to Renick and the dragon. "Okay, step three." She set to work binding the splints to the dragon's wing, using more bandages extracted from her bag. "Can you get him to fold his wing?"

Renick slid his hand along the joint where the wing met the dragon's body. At first the dragon did not respond to the touch, but eventually he folded his wing to lay flat against his body. Lainey tied the wing in place. "So he can't move it around," she explained. Sitting back, she declared she was done.

"Good," Thane said. "Now that the two of you have wasted the day fixing a broken wing, can we please continue on our journey? I prefer to keep to one hopeless task at a time."

Renick stood and tried to carry the dragon, but its scales bit into his arms and the dragon's claws started tearing his shirt.

"Here." Thane handed Renick his emptied rucksack. "Give me yours."

Placing the injured dragon on the ground, Renick stripped off his pack and handed it to Thane. The older boy started filling it with the things he had dumped out of his own.

Carefully, Renick and Lainey maneuvered the dragon into the pocket and onto Renick's back.

"How's that?" Lainey asked. "Does it bother your shoulder?"

Renick shook his head. "I'll be fine."

"Now?" Thane asked.

"Yes, Thane, now," Lainey answered, and the four of them headed back into the woods.

Kind, Brave and Trusted

Up and down Plyth bumped. Something held him in. Trapped. The rain patted on his head. Plyth opened his eyes, waking from sleep. A crack by his nose helped him see light. He smelled wet earth.

Mother?

The moving stopped, followed by a big bump that made his wing hurt. *Pain.* The crack grew to be more light and more smells. Trees, tall trees, all around. Plyth sniffed the air. Rain, dirt, tree, and a new smell. New smell made his heart beat fast. Familiar, but strange. *Alone. Scared.*

A face appeared. It was soft and round and white like a doe. The face smiled. The two-legged doe moved away. She went to stand by two others. They all smelled like the new smell. Bald bear growled at two-legged doe. He turned and pointed. Two-legged doe tilted her head to the side. Angry. They turned to the tailless squirrel. He chattered at them. Bald bear crossed his paws. Grumpy. Two-legged doe wiggled her head. Bald bear stomped around and picked up broken pieces of trees.

Where Mother?

Tailless squirrel and two-legged doe got out a big leaf. They used their odd paws to make it much bigger. Biggest leaf Plyth had ever seen. They put leaf between two trees. Tailless squirrel looked in brown lump. Two-legged doe's face came close. She rubbed under chin. Plyth liked that. But he still missed Mother. He tried to call for her. No answer.

Afraid. Plyth wiggled and tried to get out. Wing did not work right.

Two-legged doe patted his head and cooed softly. He felt his worry get smaller. Calm again, he watched. Two-legged doe sat and looked at others, smiling. Two-legged doe was kind. Kind patted Plyth on the head. Bald bear growled at her and pointed to a pile of broken trees.

Kind knelt by the pile. She breathed fire on the broken trees. But not like Plyth's fire. She used her paws. The fire stayed on the broken trees. It got bigger and bigger. Plyth was cold. The fire was too far away. He tried to get closer. But he was still held tight. He could not get away. *Trapped.*

Tailless squirrel saw Plyth and came over. Carried Plyth over to fire. Fear got less. It was nice by fire. Warm, very warm. Tailless squirrel passed around bad-smelling lumps. They ate them. *Yuck.*

A sharp crack. *Danger?*

Bald bear stood and faced the forest bravely. The brave bald bear stood ready to protect them. Plyth sniffed the air. Only a rabbit. Brave sat back down and went back to eating. He grumbled at Kind and the tailless squirrel.

Brave and Kind looked at tailless squirrel a lot. They also growled and cooed at him. He would chatter back. When they were done eating, they moved under the big leaf. Kind carried Plyth. Kind and Brave lay down. Their sounds became louder. Sleeping.

Tailless squirrel patted Plyth's head. He felt good; he trusted the tailless squirrel. Everything would be fine. *Safe.* Plyth settled down to sleep. He liked his new friends: Kind, Brave, and Trusted.

The Wall of Water

Renick watched his feet slosh in the mud. Water seeped in through holes along the side of the soles. His hand-me-down boots, threadbare and falling apart, were not meant for traipsing through the forest after a good, long rain. At least the rain had stopped. The sun now peeked down through the occasional gray cloud and reflected off the pools of water that formed in Lainey's footprints. He shifted the pack on his back to give his sore shoulder a rest. The sleeping baby dragon huffed in protest. The dragon's hot breath warmed the back of Renick's neck. He wondered, briefly, if the dragon would breathe on his frozen feet.

Up ahead, Lainey's feet stopped and turned toward him. Renick looked up. She was watching him, a concerned look on her face.

"How's our little one?" Lainey asked.

"Sleeping."

"And your shoulder?"

He shrugged and tried not to wince at the movement. "Fine."

Lainey's eyes and nose scrunched together, but she did not press further. Instead, she waited for Renick to catch up with her. She turned to walk beside him. Peering at the baby dragon, she cooed softly. Renick watched Lainey as she tickled the dragon under its chin. It huffed again and tried to settle deeper into the relative safety of the rucksack.

With a thud, Renick collided with Thane's back. The force nearly sent Thane sprawling to the ground, but with an awkward hop-jump, he caught himself. Renick managed to keep his balance by using a nearby tree trunk for support. A silvery giggle, like tinkling glass, filled Renick's ears. Lainey had her hands wrapped around her stomach as if she were squeezing a belly laugh down to a giggle. Clearing his throat, Thane turned and glared at Renick.

"Sorry," Renick said with a shrug.

Thane waved his hand at Renick and told him to be quiet. "Do you hear that?"

"What?" Lainey asked, her giggle fading. Thane shushed her.

In the silence of the rain-drenched forest, Renick could hear the faint sound of rushing water. Lainey's eyes widened— she must have heard it too.

"A river?" Renick wondered.

Thane nodded. "I think so. This could be the Hodine River."

"The one that comes from the Thormic Mountains and runs past Trevinni?" Renick asked.

Lainey gasped. "If it is, then all we need to do is follow it!"

Renick started moving forward again, this time at a quicker pace. All he could think of was how the river could lead them out of the forest. He heard Thane start to say something, but ignored him. They could be out of the forest and back home in a few days. Renick felt a pit form in his stomach as he remembered that he was not going home. He was going to Trevinni to apprentice with his uncle. He did not want to dwell on it.

As Renick neared the river, the sound of the water grew louder and louder. He emerged from the cover of the trees and shielded his eyes against the sunlight dancing along the rippled surface of the river. Brown water, littered with branches, flew past him. The ground on either side of the churning depths was flooded well over the natural bank.

"Swollen by the rains," Thane said from behind him.

"Well, we can't cross it here," Lainey declared. She sounded slightly out of breath.

"We don't need to cross it." Thane smirked.

"We don't?" Lainey placed her hands on her hips and glared at Thane.

Thane shook his head, his damp hair flopping oddly around his head. "If we follow the river upstream, we should come out of the forest on the outside bank of the river."

"Upstream?"

"Yes," Renick answered. "The river loops past Trevinni and comes back into the forest. So upstream is the way to go."

Lainey mouthed "Oh." She looked at the river and a small smile spread on her face. "Do you think the others are in Trevinni? Do you think they're okay?"

Renick could not answer. He hoped Lainey's aunt and Thane's friend were all right. It was possible that they landed safely somewhere else. But he could not be sure, and he did not want to give Lainey false hope. Before Renick could form a reply, Thane answered.

"Getting back to Trevinni is the best way to find them."

"All right then, we follow the river." Renick turned as he spoke and started trudging along beside the overfilled river. They walked for some time. He lost himself in the rhythm of his footsteps.

A squishing noise followed by a wet thud and a surprised grunt drew Renick back from where his mind had wandered. He stopped and turned to look behind him. Thane lay on the ground, propped up on his elbows in the middle of a large mud puddle. He looked up, his eyes glaring darkly from under his muddy bangs. Lainey chuckled softly and extended her hand to him. Thane hesitated for a moment, turning his eyes away from her. After a few sighs, he relented. As Thane pulled on Lainey to right himself, she too lost her footing and fell smack down in the mud. She sat there with her shoulders shaking. Renick was unsure what to do; Thane just stared at Lainey with a dumbfounded look on his face.

Lainey's bubbly laugh burst out. She slapped the mud with the flat of her hand and wiggled her feet. Renick exchanged a look with Thane. Lainey's laughter was so contagious, it did not take long for Renick to follow suit. Thane's lips twitched before he finally let a deep laugh escape his strict demeanor.

Renick was completely absorbed in the mirth of the moment when an odd sound distracted him. He stopped laughing and cocked his head, listening. The sound came again. It was a small, thin gurgle with a light hiss at the end. Renick turned his head and heard the sound once more. With a start, he realized it was coming from the dragon.

"What?" Lainey asked as she wiped tears from her cheek with a clean spot on her sleeve.

"I think ..." Renick started. He paused and took the rucksack from his back. Pulling the flap back, he stared at the dragon. It looked up at him with dark eyes and made the sound again. "I think the dragon's laughing."

"What?" Lainey knelt down next to the dragon, still huddled in its pack, and scrutinized it. The dragon had grown silent and peered at Lainey curiously.

"Dragons don't laugh," Thane said. Lainey looked up at Renick and rolled her eyes. She turned her head over her shoulder and stuck her tongue out at Thane. "What?"

"Come on, let's get going. I would like to find a nice spot to dry out," Lainey said. She stood and picked up the pack. "Can I carry him for a while?" she asked Renick. The tone of her voice made her sound small.

"Sure."

Lainey put the pack on backwards so she could cradle the injured dragon. She whispered to it as she set off to follow the river again.

Renick turned to glare at Thane.

"What?" the older boy asked. "They don't. Do they?"

"My father says that dragons are born with a sense of humor. How else would they put up with our silly antics?"

Renick answered.

"You believe that?" Thane had a smirk on his face. No doubt he had a quick response on the tip of his tongue.

"Does it matter? Lainey does." With that, he turned and followed after Lainey. After a while, he heard Thane's footsteps behind him.

They started the slow march again. Lainey's flute-like voice rose just above the sound of the rushing river as she sang happily to the baby dragon. The gentle music broke up the monotony of the long walk and Renick was grateful for it, even if Lainey was a little out of tune.

"You think she's mad at me?" Thane asked.

Renick jumped a little in surprise. He had not noticed Thane walking so close, and the question seemed odd. "I don't know. I think you just hurt her feelings a bit."

"Hurt her feelings? Over a stupid dragon?"

"She's a girl, Thane." Renick sighed. "They have silly feelings about a lot of stupid things."

"How do you know so much about girls?"

"I have three younger sisters, and two older. I'm the baby brother and so I always got way too much attention from them." Renick smiled to himself at the fond, if annoying, memories.

"I just have an older brother," Thane commented. "And my dad. And Grahm."

"Who's Grahm?"

"He's kind of like my teacher. He was the one traveling with me," Thane answered.

Renick nodded.

"Grahm was taking me to Trevinni to train as a dragon knight." Thane seemed distracted. Renick wondered if he was worried about Grahm.

"I'm going to apprentice with my uncle," Renick said, trying to divert Thane's attention.

"Doesn't your father own a dragon ranch? I would've thought you would work there."

Renick shrugged. "I have four older brothers. There's not

much space for me there."

Thane gave a half smile. "I see."

They walked side by side for a while, listening to Lainey sing. Soon Renick could no longer hear the melodic rise and fall of the song. At first he thought her voice was trailing off, and then he realized that the sound of rushing water was growing louder and louder. A sinking feeling settled into his stomach and still the sound grew louder until it was like a roar of thunder. Up ahead, Lainey climbed to the top of a hill. She stopped suddenly. Just as Renick was about to reach her, she turned back, a stricken look on her face. She held out one arm to point behind her. Renick followed the line of her finger and the sinking feeling turned to despair.

Their way was blocked by a large waterfall. Before them was a sheer face of rock reaching up into the sky. The river rushed over the side and on past them.

Thane came up beside him and said something, but Renick could not make out the words. He shook his head and pointed to his ears. "I can't hear you!" he shouted as loudly as he could. Thane moved closer.

"We'll have to climb," Thane said. Renick could tell he was shouting too, but the words were almost drowned out again.

Renick turned and examined the cliff to the side of the waterfall. The wall shot straight up, and the rocks were mostly smooth and wet. Turning back to Thane, he shook his head. "I don't think we can. At least, I can't with my sore shoulder."

Someone tapped his arm. Renick turned to look at Lainey. She got Thane's attention too before shouting. "Look!" She pointed to the other side of the river. Renick saw that over there, the ground sloped upward to the falls. That passage would be much easier.

"We'd have to turn back and find a safer place to cross," Renick said.

Thane shook his head. "It's the wrong direction."

"Renick and I can't climb that, and who knows how long it'll take us to go around." Lainey had to take a deep breath after she spoke as she struggled to be heard over the sound of the falls.

Thane crossed his arms.

"We could get lost," Lainey insisted. "We have a landmark—we should stick to it."

"I agree," Renick said. "Let's go back. There may be somewhere to cross further down."

Thane opened his mouth to object. Lainey turned to Renick. Her eyes were narrowed and her lips pressed close together. Renick shrugged his shoulders at her. She jerked her head in Thane's direction.

Renick took a deep breath and clenched his fists. "I think we should turn back!" he shouted. Without waiting for any further discussion, he turned and walked resolutely back the way they had come.

Dragons Don't Talk

Renick stomped his foot down a little harder than necessary, causing the damp dirt to form little mountains around his boot. He focused on the way the dirt rippled and cracked, but it did not work. He could still hear Thane and Lainey behind him.

"What's wrong, little one?" Lainey said.

"Do you have to keep talking to it like it understands you or something?" Thane retorted.

"I can talk to him however I want." Lainey paused for a moment and Renick thought maybe she would leave it at that. But of course, she did not. "Besides, I'm sure you talk to those hunting dogs you keep blathering on about," she added.

"Hounds. They're called hoounndss." Thane sounded the word out like he was trying to teach Lainey how to spell it. "And I don't actually expect them to respond. Other than to my commands."

"Well, can you train your dog to do this?" Lainey started humming a snappy tune. Every so often, she would skip a note. To Renick's surprise, the dragon would chime in, filling in the gaps.

Thane snorted. "So what? That's just a dumb old parlor trick. Any parrot can do that."

Lainey drew in a sharp breath. "How dare you say such a thing, Thane Shaytorrin. You apologize this instant." She stamped her foot.

"What? To a stupid dragon? No way."

Finally silence. Renick closed his eyes and puffed out his breath. He guessed the tension between Thane and Lainey was because they were tired, or hungry. At the thought, his stomach grumbled. Renick's respite was short-lived as Lainey stalked past him, her mouth in a grim line and her eyes narrowed.

"Stupid boy," she mumbled under her breath.

Renick stopped and watched her walk up the path, kicking at rocks.

"She's so emotional," Thane said with an exasperated sigh.

Renick shrugged to avoid having to say anything. He actually agreed with Lainey, but he could not admit that to Thane.

Thane looked up at the sky. "I think we've dawdled enough, don't you? We should turn back now."

Lainey's blond hair swirled around her shoulders as she whipped her head around. "We don't have to listen to you, Thane," she called.

"We'll find a crossing," Renick said. He tried to hide the fact that his confidence was fading with every step. Back at the falls, he had felt that following the river would be the best course. Now he was not so sure. But he could not let the others know, especially Thane. He could not stand the thought of losing more of the older boy's esteem. Lainey believed in him—maybe that was enough.

"Hey," Lainey called. She had set the pack with dragon on the ground and stood with her arms crossed, tapping her foot impatiently.

"What?" Thane demanded.

"The baby dragon's hungry," she announced, pointing to the rucksack at her feet. The baby dragon had his gray-blue head pocking up, the flap covering one ear. It watched Renick expectantly.

"How do you know that? Did the dragon sing it to you?" Thane jabbed. Lainey rolled her eyes and flicked her hand at him.

Renick sighed. "Lainey," he put his hand on her shoulder, "why don't you and I feed the baby dragon. We've a few strips of jerky we could soften."

Lainey shook her head back and forth, her hair floating around it. "He doesn't like the jerky. It smells funny."

Thane threw his hands in the air. "Now she's a dragon whisperer. What? Did the little lizard complain about the jerky?"

Lainey's eyes shone with tears. "Maybe he did," she said, half-heartedly.

"Dragons can't talk," Thane said.

"Thane." Renick was surprised that he was able to keep his voice neutral. "We could all use a good meal. Maybe you could catch us some rabbits?"

Thane clenched his fists.

"You are, after all, a superior hunter, and I'd love some rabbit." Lainey flashed Thane a smile and fluttered her eyelashes.

It took Renick a second to catch up with her sudden change in mood. Before Renick could collect his thoughts again, Thane was nodding his head. Thane placed one hand on the hilt of his sword and the other on his hip. "I *am* an excellent hunter. Wait here—I shall find us some dinner." He moved off into the forest.

Renick watched with his mouth hanging open. He turned to Lainey, who smiled and twirled her hands in a fancy shrug.

"My aunt says men need their egos stroked every now and then. And that they like making pretty girls happy." She looked back after Thane. "At least she was right about the first half."

Based on the evidence, Renick could not argue against that. Instead, he bent down and patted the dragon on the head.

Lainey nudged his shoulder. "A good friend would say, 'She's right about both. You're a very pretty girl, Lainey.'" Her tone was stern, but there was a twinkle in her eye.

"I guess I'm a dismal friend, then," Renick replied, trying to sound just as serious. "Do you think I'd be better at making camp?"

Lainey smiled and together they set up the shelter and started a fire. It was not long before Thane returned with two freshly killed rabbits. He held them out to Lainey, who squealed and clapped her hands before taking them. She looked down at the rabbits and back up at Thane, her face slightly green.

Thane snorted. "Would you like me to clean them for you?"

"Yes, please." She beamed.

Thane took the rabbits and cleaned them with expert hands. "Did a lot of rabbit hunting back at my father's estate. A knight often has to survive on his own in the wild, even during times of peace."

"You must've gone hunting with your father a lot," Lainey commented.

Thane's eyes narrowed slightly. "Not with my father—with Grahm."

"Grahm?" Lainey said.

"From the passenger basket," Thane explained.

"Ah." Lainey laid her chin on her bent knees. "When I lived with my aunt and uncle in Sovertin, we ate rabbit several times a week. My uncle was pretty handy with a snare, and it kept our bellies full during the winter."

"I didn't know your aunt was married," Thane said as he removed the last bit of pelt from the second rabbit.

"Different aunt," Lainey explained. "I've lived with a lot of different relatives. Aunt Melatheen took me in just a few months ago. She kind of rescued me."

"Rescued you from what?" Thane asked.

"How're we going to cook the rabbits?" Lainey asked, ignoring Thane's question.

"On a spit," Thane said.

"We don't have a spit," Lainey countered.

They both turned to look at Renick. He stood from where he sat watching their exchange. "How about I build one?"

Renick found a suitable roasting stick rather quickly. The small, fallen branch was already pointed at one end, which would be good for skewering the rabbits. Finding the two support sticks proved to be a little more difficult. The forks had to be just right and far enough down to hold the roasting stick above the fire. He had wandered so far from their small camp that he could no longer hear the sound of Lainey and Thane bantering back and forth. He turned back, not wanting to get lost. He looked up and inspected the branches of the trees as he passed them. Eventually he was able to find two suitable branches, but he had to rip them from the trees.

When Renick returned to camp, Lainey and Thane were quiet.

"What now?" Renick asked.

"Dragons can't talk," Thane said.

"Well, this one can," Lainey said. She stuck her tongue out at Thane.

Thane opened his mouth to speak, but stopped. Slowly, he reached with one hand and drew his knife. With his eyes locked on Lainey, he took aim. She screeched.

"Quiet!" Thane hissed. "And don't move."

Lainey froze mid-scream. With a flick of his wrist, Thane sent the blade flying. It landed right between the eyes of a large snake. Lainey twisted her head around and the rest of her scream escaped. The serpent writhed for a few seconds before collapsing and going completely limp.

"I caught us dessert." Thane smiled.

"Eww!" Lainey scurried to get further away from the snake.

Renick could not help himself any longer. He started laughing, breaking his silence and drawing Thane and Lainey's attention. "Lainey," Renick said when he had gained a little more control, "we aren't really going to eat it."

"We aren't?" Her voice was fearful and pleading.

"No," Thane said with a smile, "its meat is poisonous."

Relief showed on Lainey's face. "Good. Renick, did you make a spit?"

Renick nodded his head and handed one of the support

sticks he had found to Thane, who drove it into the ground next to their fire. Renick had to try a few times before he could get the other one into the ground directly across from it. Thane picked up the roasting stick and pushed the pointy end through the first rabbit.

"Wait," Renick said. "Dragons eat their meat raw. Give me some of that second rabbit."

Thane cut the rabbit in half with his knife and handed the rump end to Renick. He put the other half on the skewer and set it across the two support sticks.

"Can I borrow your knife?" Renick asked. Thane flipped the knife so he was holding the tip of the blade and held it out to Renick, who cut the rabbit into small pieces.

"What're you doing?" Lainey asked.

"The dragon's still too small to eat on his own. At this age, the mother dragon would still be partially digesting his food for him. But if we cut up the meat small enough, he'll be able to manage." Renick held out a handful of meat to Lainey. After a moment's hesitation, she took it.

"You must've fed a lot of baby dragons," she said.

Renick shrugged. "Every once in a while, there's a runt that needs hand-feeding. That usually fell to me."

"So, how do I do it?"

"Hold one little piece over his head. When he opens his mouth, drop it on his tongue, not down his throat." Renick explained.

As Lainey fed it, the baby dragon started to wiggle around and seemed to sigh contentedly.

"You look like you have something on your mind, Renick," Lainey said without raising her eyes.

"I was just remembering a story."

"Let's hear it then," Thane said gruffly. Lainey shot a dagger-like look at him. "What?" He raised his hands in surrender. "I knew you were going to ask. I just beat you too it." They both turned to watch Renick expectantly.

"A long time ago, there was a boy called Louren, who rescued a dragon that had been rejected by its mother," Renick started. He knew this tale well, as his father had told it many times. "The dragon was so grateful for what Louren had done that he stayed by his side day and night, protecting him. When Louren grew into a man, the dragon would follow him to market, where no one dared to cheat him. No thief ever stepped foot on his land. No bandits ever gave him trouble. Louren had a long and successful life. When his hair turned gray and his body started to fail, the dragon gave him a final gift. The dragon spoke Louren's name and then surrendered his life to Louren. With his body restored to its youth, Louren was able to live a second life that was just as plentiful as the first."

His tale finished, Renick looked up from the fire to see Thane and Lainey still watching him. The daylight had faded and their faces glowed against the darkness.

"I like that story," Lainey said with a yawn.

"It's just a story. Dragons don't really speak," Thane insisted.

Renick shrugged. "They don't." But he wished in his heart that they did.

The River Rushes On

Lainey looked up at the canopy of trees. Sunlight danced across the wet leaves, making them sparkle. She breathed in the refreshing scent of the forest after a rain. Aunt Melatheen loved the rain. The thought brought a pang of worry and regret. Lainey let herself feel it for a just a moment before carefully tucking it away. The best thing to do for her aunt was to get out of the forest and find help.

"Look," Thane called out.

She turned to follow the line of Thane's outstretched arm. Up ahead, the river widened to fill a large gap in the forest. The river was so flooded that it lapped at the trunks of some of the trees that lined its banks. Here the river flowed at a much lazier pace. It seemed to trickle along, spreading out and taking its time. The rushing sound had also quieted to just above a whisper. Lainey caught her breath and soaked in the peaceful moment, saving it for later.

"Do you think we can cross here?" she asked.

Thane's brown eyes scanned the river, his brow furrowed in concentration. "I think so," he said as he rubbed the stubble that had formed on his square jawline.

Lainey turned to Renick, to whom she had really been speaking. "What do you think, Renick?"

He shrugged like he always did when he was unsure. "It looks safe enough." He glanced over at Thane as he spoke, a question on his face.

To keep from laughing, Lainey pressed her lips together. It was just too much fun to make Renick squirm. Thane took a deep breath and clenched his fists. It was a bonus that it annoyed Thane as well.

Some bushes nearby rustled, the sound breaking through the calming melody of the river. The boys turned to watch the spot. Thane's hand went to his sword.

"I think if we're going to cross here, we should do it quickly." Thane was trying to sound tough and brave, but she saw his feet shifting nervously. A knot formed in Lainey's throat. If Thane was really that worried, there was something to be worried about.

"Why?" Lainey asked. When the question came out shaky, she mentally kicked herself for letting the fear leak out. She really was trying to be strong, like the boys.

"This'll be a good watering hole for the animals of the forest, which means there'll be predators lurking about," Thane answered.

"Yep. All right, then, shall we cross there?" Renick pointed to the widest part of the river. A sister knot formed in Lainey's stomach. Renick was feeling unsettled too. Were they really in that much danger? She was glad for her grip on the baby dragon's pack because it meant the boys could not see her hands shaking.

Thane nodded. "As good a place as any. I'll go first to make sure it's safe." Thane stripped off his sword as he spoke. He also pulled the knife from his boot. Holding the weapons above his head, Thane started to cross the river.

Lainey watched him intently. At the midway point, the water rose to his thighs. She could feel her breathing speed up. The water would be up to her waist. She could not swim. She opened her mouth to tell Renick as much and closed it again. They had to cross the river and it was silly for her to be afraid. After all, she could still walk across—she would not have to swim.

Renick turned to face her, his arms outstretched. "Let me take the dragon."

Lainey tilted her head and looked at him sideways. She smiled and said, "I can carry him—he's not that heavy. Plus, you'll be the rear guard. It wouldn't do to have you burdened by a passenger."

He seemed unconvinced, so she did not give him a chance to argue further. Lainey took her first step into the river. The water soaked through her thin travel shoes. The cold cut into her feet and legs as she trudged deeper into the water. At first, she kept her eyes on Thane, who was waiting on the far bank, but then her feet went numb. She had to keep her head down, watching where she stepped through the murky water.

The gentle push of the current against her legs made Lainey falter and her foot came down on a loose rock. She felt herself tilting dangerously close to the water. Throwing her hands out, she managed to steady herself. She took a few deep breaths to quiet her drumming heartbeat. When she felt ready to continue, she wrapped her arms back around the baby dragon, who had started to squirm, and took another step forward. She felt her foot slip on a slime-covered rock and went down.

The cold water of the river surrounded Lainey. The only sound that broke through the din of the rapids was the plaintive pleas of the baby dragon. Lainey felt the water close around her head. Yanking the pack off her arms, she pushed the baby dragon up toward the surface. Something pulled against her arms, and her head broke above the crushing water. Lainey sucked in a breath before she was tugged under again.

Around her there was blackness, sliced up by the light dancing across her face. The bitter cold pressed in around her. Her lungs began to ache for want of air. She kicked mightily with her legs, trying to gain control of her movement, to drive herself upward. She kept her arms extended, if nothing else, she knew she must keep the baby dragon above the surface. Just when she felt sure she would die in the cold wet of the river, her head broke the surface once more.

A voice was calling out to her, but the words were swallowed by the cold water.

Lainey felt a sob threatening to escape her tightly closed mouth. *All is not lost. All is not lost,* she told herself over and over. She would not give up yet. Thane and Renick would save her. They would come for her.

Suddenly she felt a warm comfort, much like hope, spread through her. Lainey had the distinct impression in her mind of the baby dragon wrapping its wings around her and lifting her up.

Air. She breathed deeply and looked down to see the dragon still trapped in the pack, watching her.

Then the water again.

All is not lost.

An arm wrapped around her waist and pulled her upwards.

"I've got you," Renick said in her ear.

Lainey relaxed and sobbed in between deep, desperate breaths. She pulled the baby dragon close to her and watched the brown and green blur of the forest. There was a flash of color in the trees. Lainey tried to focus on the movement, blinking the water from her eyes. Thane's figure appeared, sprinting along the bank. The fear and panic receded as she watched him move through the trees. She was safe.

The pressure of Renick's arm around her chest lessened and she slipped below the water again.

Lainey felt the rucksack with the baby dragon being pulled away from her. She clutched it closer, but her hands were too cold and she lost her grip. Looking up, she saw the sunlight play off the surface of the water. Two long shadows descended toward her. Strong hands gripped her shoulders and she surfaced again.

Sucking in gulps of air, Lainey tried to speak as Thane dragged her out of the river. All that came out was a fit of coughs. "Dragon," she managed to wheeze. Thane's step did not falter as he carried her away from the edge of the water. Lainey stretched out one hand over Thane's shoulder and said with more strength, "The dragon!"

"Got him." Renick's lanky frame rose from a shallow section of the river just a little downstream. He held the soaked pack and the wriggling baby dragon.

Lainey sighed with relief. "Oh!" she exclaimed, "and Renick! Sorry, I forgot about you," she added with a sheepish smile.

Thane laughed. Lainey could feel it rumbling through his chest as he set her on the ground. The gentle movement helped erase some of the lingering fear.

Renick gave her a half smile. "It's okay, Lainey."

"We need to get her warm," Thane said. Renick nodded, set the dragon down next to Lainey, and dodged off into the woods.

"Where's—s h—he g—going?" Lainey asked, her teeth chattering.

"To collect firewood. We need to get you out of your wet cloak." He helped her unclasp her traveling cloak and pull her arms out of the sleeves. Thane laid the cloak over a nearby branch. When he returned, he draped his mostly dry cloak around her shoulders.

Lainey tried to offer thanks, but the only sound she managed to make was a vague grunt. She smiled up at him instead.

There was a soft thud and Lainey looked down to see that the baby dragon had knocked the pack over as it attempted to get out. She reached down and tried to aid him with her numb fingers. After a moment of her fumbling, Thane sighed and gently covered her frozen hands with his. They were so warm that they almost burned against her skin. He moved her hands aside, peeled the baby dragon from the rucksack, and placed it in Lainey's outstretched arms.

"Thanks," she said. Thane looked as if he were about to say something, but Renick returned with the firewood.

The two boys set to work building the fire. Once they had a good blaze going, they helped Lainey move to sit next to it. The baby dragon started crooning as it warmed by the fire. Lainey laughed. It felt good to laugh after the terrifying trip down the river. Thane and Renick joined her, their laughs blending oddly with hers. Even the baby dragon started making short barking noises. Lainey stroked the dragon's neck.

"It's okay," she whispered softly. "We're safe now."

Run!

Something wrong. Plyth lifted his head. The fire warmed his cold, wet scales. *Something out there.* He turned his head and searched. Kind rubbed his head, but it did not comfort him. He wiggled in her lap. *Yes, something wrong.*

Plyth sniffed the air. Wood. Green. Rain. Rabbit. Smoke. He smelled all that. Nothing bad. Good smells. Plyth listened. Kind hummed a sweet, soft song. Good sound. Plyth liked humming. Wind moved some leaves. Rabbit darted away. Dirt shifted.

He stopped. Dirt moved? Why? Under a foot. Plyth tasted the air again. Nothing. No bad smell.

Snap.

Plyth jumped out of Kind's lap. Looking, looking everywhere. Listen, smell. Wind again—this time it smelled of something familiar. Something Plyth smelled before. Something from when his mother fell. Bad smell, very bad smell. *Danger.*

Hunters.

Plyth ran in a circle. Whined, and ran in a circle again. Hunters. There were hunters nearby. It was not safe here.

Kind picked up Plyth and rubbed him. He tried to wiggle free. *Scared.* Need to run away. He whined again. *Bad.* Hunters bad. Danger—must get away. Hurt mother—now they want to hurt him. Plyth cried. Kind held him tighter. She said something. She was worried. Trusted felt unsure. Brave was tense.

Hunters. Danger.

Plyth looked at Trusted. *Run away*. He wanted to get away. Plyth looked at Kind. She not understand. How to tell? How to tell?

More dirt shifted. They were coming. Close now. They must have trail to follow. Must see them, hear them. Maybe they could still get away.

Plyth's fear got worse. He wanted to fly away, He beat his wings. *Pain*. He could not fly. Broken wing. He wiggled again, trying to get out of Kind's grasp. *Need to run*. Kind stood up. Plyth arched his neck back and tried to see her eyes. Needed to tell her. *Run. Run. Run*. Mother would know. Mother could tell.

Brave and Trusted went to woods. No, not safe. *Come back—hunters that way*. They gone for long time. Plyth wiggled some more. *Not that way. Not safe*. Trusted came back, and Brave came back too. They okay. They growled and chattered at Kind.

Plyth thought of Kind, then thought of running away. He thought of danger and made his thoughts big. Loud. *Run. Run*. "Run!"

Kind made a funny sound. Lots of air going in at once. Plyth made thought loud and big and looked at Brave and Trusted. *Run. Run*. "Run!"

Trusted looked at Plyth. He chattered at Kind and Brave.

They started running. Yes, yes. *Run!*

Dragon's Voice

Renick burst through the trees into a small clearing. They were exposed. He needed to find cover. Off to his left, toward the edge of the open space, an ancient tree had fallen over and rotted out. The remains were large enough to hide them. Renick changed course and headed for the tree. When he reached it, he skidded to a halt. Lainey whipped past him, sliding to the ground, her back to the log and her arms clutching the baby dragon.

"You okay?" Renick asked through gasps of air.

Lainey nodded. She was breathing too hard to speak.

Turning, Renick scanned the line of trees. Thane leapt into the clearing and pivoted, sword drawn. He stood ready, the point of his blade swaying back and forth. Then he spun around, and in a few short bounds, dodged behind the log.

"I don't think they followed us," Thane said as he sheathed his sword. He crouched down and knelt on one knee.

Renick crumpled to the ground next to Lainey. He sat with his legs folded and picked at the long weeds that covered the ground.

Looking up, Lainey asked, "Did you hear him ..."

"Talk?" Renick finished with a nod.

A smile broke across Lainey's face. "I thought I was losing

my mind."

"You already had," Thane jibed.

Lainey looked at him sideways. Renick could not tell if he was joking or not until the corner of Thane's mouth twitched. Lainey flicked her hand in Thane's direction as if to dismiss him.

"He can talk." Renick shook his head. A talking dragon. He remembered lying awake in bed at night listening to the grunts and groans of sleeping dragons and wondering what they meant. Renick could smell the straw of the brooder where he held hatchlings and stared into those intelligent eyes, wondering what was behind them. And now, sitting here in front of him, was a talking dragon. "He can talk."

Lainey closed her mouth and looked at him. Apparently she had been saying something to Thane. "Yes, Renick," she said gently.

"He can talk," Renick repeated.

"Renick, I think you've established that. Now can we please move on?" Thane popped his head up and looked over the log as he spoke.

Renick nodded, but added under his breath, "He can talk," one more time.

"I wonder what his name is." Lainey removed the dragon from the pack and peered into his eyes. "Huh, little guy?" The dragon just cocked his head at her.

A wave of curiosity hit Renick. It was familiar, yet foreign. Like when his brothers told his father's stories. The words were the same, but the voice was different. Renick studied the baby dragon.

Curious, the baby dragon seemed to say in Renick's mind.

"It doesn't understand what you're saying," Thane said.

"Quiet," Renick said. "Do you …" He shrugged. "Do you feel that?"

Lainey nodded. "He's curious."

Thane shook his head. "Seriously, you two have lost it."

"No, she's right. Pay attention and you might be able to feel it too." Renick moved to sit next to Lainey. "Let's try to figure out his name again."

"What's your name?" she asked the dragon. He tilted his head the other way.

Confused.

Thane's brow furrowed.

"Hah! You do feel it!" Lainey pointed an accusing finger at Thane.

Thane closed his eyes. "All right, so I do. Big deal."

Lainey exchanged a look with Renick and rolled her eyes. She focused on the baby dragon again. "Maybe we should try showing him what we mean. I'm Lainey ..."

Kind.

Lainey blinked a few times. "Thank you, I think. But I don't understand." She turned the dragon so he was looking at Thane. "And this is Thane. He's not as mean as he looks."

Brave.

"And this is Renick," Lainey said, swiveling the dragon again.

Trusted.

"That's odd," Renick said. "I wonder what he means by kind, brave, and trusted."

"Plyth," the baby dragon hissed.

Thane leaned closer. "Did he just say 'plyth'?" he asked.

"I think so," Lainey said. "Is your name Plyth?"

"Me, Plyth," the dragon repeated.

Renick could not breathe. His heart was pounding faster than it had when they were running. A dozen stories, legends, and bits of lore that his father used to tell him crowded in his mind. They all alluded to the dragons' ability to speak. Up until this moment, Renick had thought them only fables. He had not dared to hope that they might have some truth to them.

"Well, it's nice to meet you, Plyth." Lainey smiled and hugged the dragon close to her. "Now I don't have to keep calling you 'little guy' anymore."

"Ask him if he knows who those men were back there," Thane said.

"Ask him yourself." Lainey plopped the dragon into

Thane's arms. "You've a mouth, don't you?" She crossed her arms and leaned back against the log.

"Uh, do you know who those men were?" Thane said to Plyth's tail. With a chuckle, Lainey reached out and turned Plyth so he was facing Thane.

Happy.

"I think he still isn't understanding us. Maybe if you pictured one of the men, he'd know what you meant," Renick offered.

Thane gave Renick an annoyed look.

"Here, let me do it," Renick said as he took Plyth. Renick closed his eyes and pictured one of the men he had seen in the woods. The man had long, unkempt hair the color of mud. An odd tattoo ran down the man's neck and he had a scowl on his face.

Plyth squirmed in Renick's lap. *Danger.*

"Shhh." Lainey rubbed Plyth behind the ears. "We're safe now. We just want to know who they were."

"Unthers," Plyth said.

"Unthers?" Thane spat. "That doesn't even make sense."

Lainey hit Thane's arm. "I think he means 'hunters.' He's still a baby, remember?"

Somewhere in the distance, branches rubbed up against each other. Renick held his breath, listening for signs of pursuit. The moment passed.

"I'm going to check the perimeter," Thane whispered. "You two wait here."

The air seemed thick and heavy as they waited for Thane to return. The peaceful quiet of the clearing turned menacing and every small sound amplified. Renick jumped a little when Thane reappeared.

"Sow," Thane said. "With some piglets. But they moved off the other way."

Renick let out his breath.

"What kind of hunters?" The words exploded out of Lainey like she had been holding them in.

"Dragon hunters," Renick and Thane said together.

"Dragons? You sure?"

"When I was younger, a dragon got very sick and went mad. It escaped its pen and started killing live stock. My father and some of the other men from our village had to hunt it down." Renick felt a sickening feeling in his stomach at the memory of seeing the dead dragon being dragged back to the ranch to be destroyed. "The hunters back there had similar equipment to what my father used."

"What kind of equipment?" Lainey asked.

"Nets, ropes, and at least one giant crossbow," Renick said.

"Did you see the shafts?" Thane asked.

Renick nodded. "They looked like the one that got the flyer."

Lainey gasped. "You don't think …"

"And the gray," Thane added in a harsh tone. At Renick's raised eyebrows, he said, "I took a closer look while you two were patching Plyth up."

"Why would anyone want to hunt dragons?" Lainey said, horrified. She scooped Plyth out of Renick's lap and started rocking him back and forth.

"Their hides are valuable," Renick answered. "They grow to be bigger than our dragons. And their scales are brighter in color, and stronger. My father says they also take their hearts. The stories say there is magic in a dragon's heart."

"That's gross." Lainey gagged. She looked down at Plyth. "We can't let them get him." Her words echoed Renick's thoughts.

"Well, we can't go back to the river. The hunters are blocking the way." Thane jabbed his thumb back in the direction they had come.

"Where to, then?" Lainey asked.

Renick felt a sudden chill, like a breeze coming off snow. "Mountains," Plyth said.

Thane nodded and rubbed his chin. "We could follow the mountains west. It's a little farther out of the way, and the terrain will be rougher. But at least we'd have a landmark to follow again."

"All right, then." Renick rubbed his hands together. "The mountains."

Way Station

Just a few hours' hike from the clearing, Renick noticed a brown bunch of thorny bushes. The tangled mass stood higher than a man's head and stretched out for several paces before curving out of his view.

"That's odd," Lainey remarked. She started to walk around, inspecting the wall of bushes. "Hey, there's a gap here." Renick watched Lainey disappear through the thick under-brush. She gasped. "Come on, you have to see this!"

Renick looked to Thane, who crossed his arms and shook his head. With a shrug at Thane, Renick moved through the gap. He looked around, his mouth falling open. An area large enough for a dragon flyer to land in had been cleared of undergrowth. There were a few tables and chairs, as well as the toppled remains of a few sleeping tents. At the far end there was also a small building that appeared to be a storage shed. The entire area was surrounded by thick, thorny bushes and vines—a barrier against the dangers of the forest.

"What is it?" Renick asked.

"It looks like an abandoned way station," Thane commented. "They used them before, when the passenger baskets were more cramped." He kicked at the fallen tents and sent a flurry of bugs scampering away.

Lainey wrinkled her nose. "Eww."

Renick handed Plyth to Lainey and went to investigate the storage shed. The door was hanging crooked on its hinges and when Renick pulled it open, it fell off completely. Renick scrunched his face and shoulders in anticipation of the sound. When the door crashed to the ground, he turned to Thane and Lainey with an apology on his face. They all stood quiet for a moment, waiting. Renick strained his ears for any movement through the woods around them. After several tense moments, he exhaled. "That was close," he said.

"Just be more careful," Thane said. "We don't want anything out there," he pointed to the woods, "to know that we're in here."

Lainey looked at Renick and rolled her eyes before turning away.

Renick entered the dark shed. A sliver of light from a crack in the ceiling allowed him to make out the shapes of sacks and barrels. Starting at one end and working his way around the shed, Renick inspected every sack, basket, and barrel. He found spoiled bread, wheat, and fruit. Mice had gotten to some of it. He even came across an old bird's nest. He found a few useful things: a small pot for cooking that fit in his rucksack, some dried meat to add to their stores, a long hunting knife, and a coil of rope.

Carrying his treasures, Renick ducked out of the shed and looked around for the others. Lainey was seated at the table, humming softly. Plyth sat on the table near her, his head tilting back and forth in time to her song. Thane was nearby, picking through the fallen tents and other debris.

"Look what I found," Renick pronounced, placing his finds on the table next to Plyth.

Lainey squealed and clapped her hands. "Oh, I can make us stew." She scooped up some of the dried meat and the pot and carried them to a nearby fire pit.

Thane came over to investigate. He picked up the hunting knife and examined it. "It's a good knife," he said, holding out the handle to Renick. "You should keep it."

Renick took the knife and tucked it in his belt. "Thanks. I—"

A sound much like a branch breaking in the forest made Renick stop and Thane place his hand on his sword. Plyth ducked his head and laid his ears back.

Danger.

Lainey had frozen with the small pot still in her hand, poised over the budding fire. Renick jerked his head toward Thane and Plyth, and Lainey moved stealthily to stand with them.

Thane motioned them to lean close. "I think the hunters are out there," he said, his voice barely audible.

"Hunters," Plyth hissed, mimicking Thane's tone and body language.

As if to confirm Thane's suspicions, a voice sounded from the woods. "Pick it up, men. I want to camp in the way station tonight."

Renick exchanged looks with Thane and Lainey.

"We need to get out of here," Thane whispered.

Lainey reached out and gripped Renick's arm. Her bottom lip quivered slightly. Renick extracted her fingers from his arm and gave them a reassuring squeeze. "The fire," he whispered. A light went on in Lainey's eyes, and she nodded and hurried over to the fire she had been starting.

Renick scooped up the rest of his finds and met the others at the gap in the thorny bushes. They paused while Thane poked his head out to make sure it was safe. Without looking back, Thane motioned for Renick and Lainey to follow. They moved through the forest, Thane leading them to a dense portion of trees.

They slipped behind the trees just as they heard a voice saying, "Ah, here we are."

Crouching down, Renick peered through a space between two tree trunks. The band of hunters, all eight of them, stood outside the tall, thorny bushes. Seven of them disappeared into the way station. The eighth stood watch at the gap.

Thane leaned down to Renick's ear and whispered, "He's

too close. I don't think we can move away without him seeing or hearing us."

Renick nodded in agreement. "Do you think if we sleep here, we'll be safe?"

Thane's eyes narrowed for a moment. "Yes, but we should keep watch. I'll take the first shift."

Turning, Renick relayed their plan to Lainey.

For a long time, the hunters were busy around the camp, making lots of noise and yelling, often using very foul language. At one point, Thane tapped on Renick's shoulder. Thane pointed to Lainey and then placed his hands over his ears. When Renick did not respond, Thane repeated the motion. Finally understanding, Renick turned to Lainey to tell her not to listen. She was lying on her stomach, her elbows in the dirt and her hands already clamped tightly over her ears. Just then the swearing in the camp got louder. Lainey cringed and pressed her hands tighter against her head. She gave Renick a little half smile.

After the men had made camp, they shared a meal of what smelled like hot stew. The aroma made Renick's stomach churn with jealousy. He begrudgingly passed out a few of the strips of dried meat he had found. He chewed on his half-heartedly and tried to imagine he was eating a large bowl of meaty stew like his mother made back home.

His stomach still growling, Renick sat with his back to a tree and closed his eyes. He was half asleep when Lainey nudged him. He looked over at her; Lainey pointed to the way station.

"I tell ya, there was a hatchlin' with that cow," one deep voice said.

"Well, there wasn't one by 'er carcass, and it wouldn't't've wandered away from its mum," another said.

"It might've run off with its tail between its legs," the first voice said. The hunters laughed at this.

"It'd be too young fer the Awakenin'. It'd be mute. No need to track it down," another man replied.

Something the hunters said sparked a memory, a line in a

story his father told him a long time ago. It was not like the other old stories, the ones his father told over and over. Renick had only heard it once. But it spoke of a baby dragon awakening to a new day, its mind alert and open to the world around it. He wished he could remember the exact words.

There was a *thunk* and one of the men yelped in pain. "After you shot down that flyer, you want to botch another job by leaving it unfinished?" a gruff voice asked.

Lainey gasped and clapped her hand over her mouth to silence the sound. She looked over at Thane and Renick. Renick's chest felt tight and his heart was beating fast. These dragon hunters had shot down the flyer and killed Plyth's mother. He turned to Thane, whose eyes were angry slits. "Later," Thane mouthed. Renick understood. It would be too hard to discuss this new piece of information now.

"We stick to the mission. But keep your eyes peeled for any leftovers," said the gruff voice. There were some grumbles, but no one challenged the order.

Renick settled back into his sleeping position, his head resting against the tree. He struggled to quiet the swirling questions in his mind. It was not until the hunters had found their own beds and were snoring softly in the night that Renick finally drifted off to sleep.

What felt like only a few moments passed before Thane shook Renick awake. He opened his weary eyes. "My watch?" Renick asked in a low whisper.

Thane shook his head. "They're all asleep, even the watchman." He added something under his breath. Renick did not catch it all, but it sounded like something about being lazy and putting the others at risk. "Lucky for us, though."

Renick climbed to his feet. Lainey was already standing, Plyth cradled in her arms. They moved quietly away from the way station. Thane took the lead, taking them north and toward the foothills of the mountain.

There was the sound of someone moving around in the half light, a *thunk*, a crash, and another thunk. Renick froze. The others did too. A man grumbled in his sleep, turned over, and continued snoring. After all had been quiet for several moments, Renick let out a sigh of relief. He followed the others as they started moving again. Thane pointed ahead to a stand of trees with thick bushes at their base, indicating that was where they were headed.

Renick lagged behind a little—he kept looking over his shoulder. He had the uneasy feeling that they were being watched. With his head turned to observe the way station, he took a step forward. His foot came down on a small branch and it snapped in two. He looked up and locked eyes with Lainey and Thane, their faces mirroring the fear he felt.

The sound of a body shifting indicated that someone behind the way station barrier was awake. Renick could hear his confused expressions. It sounded like he was getting up. It took less than a heartbeat for Renick to recover. He started running for the safety of the bushes they were heading toward. Lainey and Thane followed. Once he was safely crouching behind a thick bush, Renick looked back at the way station. One of the hunters emerged from the gap in the wall of thorns.

Thane and Lainey hit the ground next to Renick as they dove for cover. Plyth let out a little yelp. Thane clamped a hand over the baby dragon's snout and shushed him.

"Hurt!" Plyth tried to say around Thane's hand, but the word was muffled.

"Huh? What's that?" the hunter said. After scanning the woods around him, the hunter was just about to return when Lainey shifted her weight. Plyth cried out, the high pitched sound making it through his closed mouth.

Pain.

Renick's shoulder ached for a moment as Plyth projected his discomfort.

The hunter stopped and turned to face the bush they were hiding behind. He yelled something and started running toward them. Renick looked around frantically. There was no way for them to leave their hiding spot without being noticed. He looked down at Plyth and knew what he had to do.

Renick stood and ran back the way they had come. He was passing the trees where they had spent the night when the hunter spotted him.

"Stop!" a deep, booming voice called to him.

Renick kept running. He hoped that the others would take advantage of the distraction. He did not dare to look back. Instead, he put his head down and kept running. A set of heavy footsteps pursued him. Soon those footsteps were joined by others. Renick ran harder. Ignoring the sounds behind him, he focused on moving forward.

His foot caught on something. Renick tumbled, rolling as he went down and coming back up almost on his feet. Using his arms, he pushed himself fully upright. For a moment, he thought all would be fine. A heavy hand descended on his shoulder. Renick fell to the ground again.

The hunters surrounded him.

Renick lay still, trying to catch his breath. One of the hunters leaned over him. The man had three deep scars running parallel from his missing eye down his neck. The red lines disappeared under his shirt. "What do we have here?" the hunter asked in a gravelly voice. He pushed Renick with the toe of his heavy boot. "Speak, runt."

"I'm lost." Renick wheezed.

"Name," the hunter barked.

Renick clamped his teeth together.

"Name!" This time the command was followed up with a swift kick to his gut.

"Rub," Renick said, using the nickname his older brothers used to call him.

"Oy, he doesn't look like a dragon to me," one of the other hunters cried out.

"I tell ya, I heard it. Twice." The man Renick had seen earlier waved three fingers in the other hunter's face.

"Can you cry like a baby dragon, boy? Wah, wah," one of the hunters said as he poked Renick with the tip of a short sword. The hunters all burst into laughter.

"Silence!" the hunter with the scar said, slicing his hand

through the air. Everyone fell silent. "Gunther, tie him up. We'll take him back to camp."

The hunter who had heard Plyth—Renick assumed his name was Gunther—pulled him to his feet. Gunther turned Renick around roughly, grabbed his arms, and pulled them behind his back. The rope Gunther used was rough and scratched Renick's hands, and the hunter wrapped the rope a little tighter than was necessary around Renick's wrists.

The lead hunter, the one with the scars, pulled a knife from his belt and held it up to Renick. "I'll get your secret out one way or the other," he threatened.

The Hunters' Camp

The way station was transformed. It did not look abandoned anymore. Instead, it looked like a proper camp. The sleeping tents had been righted and the whole area was clean and orderly. The fire pit glowed with coals still hot from the night's fire. Renick could smell breakfast. Bacon, eggs, biscuits. His stomach groaned at the savory smells. Without his permission, Renick's tongue ran across his lips.

"Ah, is the runt hungry?" one of the hunters jeered. He picked up a half-eaten piece of bacon, wiggled it in front of Renick's nose, and crammed the whole thing in his mouth.

"Sit him here," the lead hunter said. The man stood over an uneven log near the fire pit, still holding his knife.

Renick felt cold sweat trickle down his neck.

"Yes, sir, Horrin." Gunther pushed him roughly down onto the log.

"Now, Rub, was it?" the lead hunter said, leaning close to Renick's face. The man's breath smelled terrible and his teeth were yellow. "Where is the baby dragon?"

"Dragon?" Renick asked.

"Yes, the baby dragon. Lost its mother a few days back. Gunther here heard it squawking just before we caught you."

"I don't know what you're talking about," Renick answered.

The leader held his knife to Renick's throat. "Is that so? Have you seen a baby dragon recently?"

"How recently?" Renick asked.

Gunther struck Renick across the face with the back of his hand. The force of the blow startled Renick and made his cheek sting.

"Enough with the smart talk! Answer my question," the lead hunter ordered, his voice dropping to a threatening tone.

"Yes. I grew up on a dragon ranch, so I see baby dragons all the time," Renick answered. To him it felt like it came out sounding funny. He rubbed the inside of his cheek with his tongue, hoping it would bring the feeling back. Gunther kicked his left shin and sharp lances of pain shot through it. He tried to hold a straight face, but a small moan of pain betrayed Renick.

"Have you seen one in the woods?" Horrin clarified.

"One what?" Renick was rewarded with another slap to the face.

"I don't have time to play with you, boy." Horrin spat in his face. "You know where that dragon is—I am sure of it. And I know you heard it talk. So, if you want to make it out of this forest alive, you'll tell me where it is!"

"Never," Renick said through clenched teeth.

Horrin smiled at him. "We shall see." Turning to Gunther, he said, "Put him over there."

"But ..." Gunther started to protest.

Horrin met the other hunter's eye—a look of silent communication passed between them. "Put him there."

"Ah," Gunther said. He nodded his head and tapped his temple. "I sees. I'll put 'im over there, shall I?"

Renick was dragged to the far side of the way station to a bare spot next to the thickest part of the thorny bush wall. Gunther threw him down on his side. "Stay put." Gunther kicked him once, then turned and walked away.

Wriggling on the ground like a worm, Renick managed to get himself onto his back. A giant crossbow caught his attention. Renick swallowed as the sun glinted off the point of one of the enormous bolts. He took a deep breath, squared his shoulders, and tried not to think about the weapon.

He turned his head to inspect the thorny bushes. At the base of one bush, there was a small gap less than two hands high. It was not much, but it was all he had. Renick lifted his head and tried to sit up. He managed to make it halfway before he fell back to the ground. Next, he tried kicking his legs to get more momentum. After a few minutes of failure, Renick changed tactics.

Using his proven method of worm wriggling, Renick got himself onto his stomach and began to crawl. He lifted his legs until his knees rested on the dirt. He pushed and slid his face against the ground. Small rocks and twigs left stinging scratches on his face, and his mouth filled with dirt. Renick continued on. Once he reached the bushes, he thrashed around a bit until he could see back into the camp. He was surprised to see that no one was watching him. He hesitated, unsure if he should continue.

Renick turned his attention back to the bush in front of him. Moving through the thorn-laden branches would be worse than inching along the dirt. For a moment, he considered abandoning the escape attempt. Thane, Lainey, and Plyth were probably far away and safe by now. He would not be able to find them, and traveling in the forest alone was dangerous.

But he had to try.

He took a deep, dust-filled breath, shifted his knees back and forth, and drove his head into the bush. Several sharp thorns bit into the back of his head and neck. His forehead, though, received most of the torment. Renick gasped, blowing a cloud of dirt around his head. The dust coated his lungs and he coughed a few times. After taking a moment to recover, Renick readied himself to move again. He pushed forward, but instead of driving further into the bush, he was pulled backwards by a pair of strong hands gripping his ankles. Panicked, Renick kicked hard, but the pressure on his ankles increased.

"Settle down, boy!" Gunther said. The hunter flipped Renick over on his back. "Thought ya might try somethin' like that. Caught ya, stupid." Gunther slapped Renick in the head and chuckled to himself. Taking Renick by one leg, Gunther pulled him to the center of the camp. He called to one of the other hunters, "Ho, Marrkit, drive me a pole righ' here." Marrkit, who sat near a freshly gathered pile of firewood, picked up a long branch about as wide as his fist.

"Here." Marrkit threw the branch at Gunther. "Drive it yerself." He returned to his drink.

Gunther dropped Renick's foot. Renick waited until he could hear the thump, thump, thump of Gunther driving the piece of wood into the ground. Not really caring where he was headed, Renick started crawling again. He had not made it very far before a hard boot on his back pressed him to the ground.

"And where do ya think ya're goin'?" Gunther's voice asked.

Renick rolled on to his back, knocking Gunther off balance. With all the strength he could muster, Renick drove his feet toward the man's face. He heard a crunch and Gunther wailed in pain. Renick laughed. The hunter sounded like a little girl.

"What's your problem?" Horrin asked as he approached.

"Da liddle brat brod my dose," Gunther complained.

"Git!" Horrin said. "I'll handle the boy."

Gunther's footsteps shuffled away.

Renick was pulled to his feet and brought face-to-face with Horrin.

The cavity where his second eye should be commanded all of Renick's attention. After a moment, he blinked and refocused. Renick spat in Horrin's good eye. The hunter recoiled and punched Renick in the gut. As he doubled over, Renick caught a glimpse of a small tattoo in the hollow of Horrin's neck. "The seeker's mark?" Renick recognized it from a book his father had shown him once.

Horrin grabbed the hair at the base of Renick's neck and yanked him forward. "I'll say this once. I've been kind thus far. If you dare to defy me again, I'll slit your throat. You're trying to play me for a fool. I know who you are, son of a dragon breeder. I'll not let you thwart me. I'll find and slaughter that dragon, and you'll help me," he promised.

"I'll die first!" Renick said.

"Oh, I'm counting on it."

Brave to the Rescue

Thane wrapped his arm around the tree branch and leaned forward to get a better view. He watched as the figures of the hunters milled about. As he marked each man's movements, Thane calculated his chances against each one. He could probably take any one of them, but that was it—just one. Stealth was his only option. Thane returned to studying the way station. In the center of the camp, near the fire pit, Renick sat tied to a stake. The boy's head was hanging low. Every once in a while, it would bob up and down or sway back and forth. Renick must be drifting in and out of consciousness. They were not too late.

With a few quick movements, Thane was back on the ground.

"Well?" Lainey asked, her gray eyes searching through the dim light.

"It'll be difficult. The place is crawling with hunters."

"How's Renick doing?"

Thane shook his head. "Not good."

Lainey rolled her hand to ask for more information, an exasperated look on her face.

"He's not fully awake—beyond that, I don't know."

Lainey bit her lip and bounced a little bit. "Okay, I can

work with that." She started digging in her healer's pouch, mumbling to herself.

"Help?" the little lizard hissed.

"No, Plyth, you're too small to help. You wait here with me," Lainey told it.

"Help," the dragon insisted. It ran over to Thane and pressed its warm snout against his leg. The baby dragon let out a little puff of air; its heat penetrated Thane's boots and warmed his skin. The world around Thane tilted and the edges of his vision blurred. He had to brace himself against the ground with one hand. When the sensation passed, Thane looked up. Everything seemed to be slightly out of focus and a dull buzz echoed in the back of his head. A quick shake cleared his vision, but the buzz remained.

"Shoo," Thane said and kicked his leg. The little lizard hobbled over to Lainey. Taking a deep breath, Thane crouched down and took a step into the darkness.

He approached the barrier around the way station slowly, taking one careful step at a time. Staying low to the ground, Thane crept to the gap in the thorny wall and peeked around it. A lone man sat the first watch. The watchman's eyes scanned the night, ever alert. The fire had burned down and the camp was shrouded in darkness.

Thane felt around in the dirt until he found a rock the size of his fist. Pulling back his arm, he lobbed the rock over the wall of bushes to the far side of the way station. When the hunter's head turned, Thane started moving. He circled around the camp to approach from the watchman's rear. His eyes stayed fixed on the hunter as Thane made his way closer to Renick.

A sleeping man at Thane's feet coughed, and the watchman spun around to look in his direction. Despite his years of training, Thane froze. His mind told him to reach for his sword, to stand and face the enemy bravely. But something held him fast. The watchman's eyes scanned over the spot where Thane crouched. Thane could hear his heartbeat pounding in his ears. After seven painfully shallow breaths, the watchman turned away.

Thane had to cover his mouth to keep from vocalizing his astonishment. The watchman had looked right at him, he was sure of it. Thane saw the firelight reflecting off the metal on his sword belt and sheath. Though not as polished as usual, it still glowed yellow against the dark night. If nothing else, that should have given him away.

He took a deep breath and absently rubbed at his leg, which felt unusually hot. What was it Grahm was always saying? Never look a gift horse in the mouth. Taking advantage of his mysterious invisibility, Thane crossed to the center of the camp and knelt beside Renick.

Thane tapped the younger boy's shoulder. Renick groaned and tossed his head a little.

Thane whispered in his ear, "It's me, Thane."

Renick shifted and pulled his head up. Weary, bloodshot eyes looked up from beneath straggly brown hair. "Thane?" he wheezed.

Placing a finger at his lips, Thane reached down and deftly pulled the knife from his boot. He used it to slice through Renick's bonds, then moved his head toward the man on watch. Renick turned his head and nodded in understanding.

"Can you stand?" Thane asked.

Renick shook his head. Thane took hold of Renick's arm and pulled it over his shoulders, wrapping his free hand around Renick's thigh. With the injured boy laying across his back, he pushed himself into a standing position. The extra weight threw him off balance and he took an involuntary step backwards. The heel of Thane's boot collided with a pot that had been resting by the fire, and it clattered softly.

The slight sound was enough. Once again, the watchman turned to look in their direction. Thane felt the breath catch in his chest, and then, with a rush, it came out. Every inch of his body tingled; his hand ached for his sword. Thane closed his eyes and stood as still as he could. To keep himself focused and to mark the passage of time, he counted silently to himself. It was a trick Grahm had taught him on a hunting trip. The idea was to keep your mind occupied without distracting it from the vigil. He reached one hundred and forty-two before the hunter spoke.

"Darn rats," the watchman grumbled. He stood and headed for the storage shed.

Thane plunged forward, moving as quickly as he dared. He had reached the gap in the thorn-laden bushes when the man appeared again, chewing on a bit of dried something. Thane swung himself through the bushes and around the barrier. He dropped to his knees, his shoulders and back aching from supporting Renick's limp form.

When he did not hear any commotion from the way station, Thane stood again and crossed quickly to the stand of trees where Lainey was waiting. She sat with her eyes fixed on the line of tall bushes. Thane laid Renick down as gently as he could. Renick groaned in protest all the same.

Lainey turned to face them and jumped a little as if she had been startled. She opened her delicate mouth to speak, but closed it again when her eyes fell on Renick. Her hands snapped into action. With one, she placed a handful of crushed leaves into Renick's partially open mouth. The other hand pressed a waterskin to Renick's lips.

"Drink," she commanded. Renick took three eager gulps before Lainey withdrew the waterskin.

Renick sat up, looking more awake and alert. "Thanks," he said in a hoarse whisper.

The baby dragon danced around them. "Plyth hide Brave. Hide."

"Get ready to run," Thane warned, reaching down and scooping up the dragon. "And you be quiet!"

Lainey helped Renick get up and they all crouched low next to the bushes.

"Oy, what's this?" the watchman exclaimed.

Thane took off running. Renick, supported by Lainey, followed next to him. Shouts echoed in the night as the hunters in the camp awoke to the watchman's alarm. "He's gone! The runt's gone!"

They had only a slight head start. They would need to find a place to hide quickly. Thane led them toward the mountain peaks that loomed ahead. Thane kept them on course with glimpses of the snowy peaks through the loose canopy. The ground beneath his feet began to slope upwards as they approached the foothills. The baby dragon squirmed a little in his grasp. Thane almost lost his hold, and after that, the dragon lay quietly in his arms. But Thane could still feel the dragon's heart racing, pulsing rapidly against his hand.

As the mountains drew nearer, the trees started to thin and the ground became more rocky. Thane's energy was waning and a quick look told him that Renick and Lainey were falling behind. He scanned the area, looking for a place to hide. Thane thought he saw the image of a cave, but it did not match the terrain around him. He blinked and the image vanished. It would have made the perfect hiding place.

The dragon started wriggling in his hands again, pulling to the right. Thane looked in that direction, and through the widening gaps in the trees, he saw a cave. When he changed directions to head for the dark opening the baby dragon leapt from his hold and bounded forward. Thane hurried to catch up, it did not take long. The dragon was sniffing around at the cave's mouth. Thane slowed to a walk and approached the dragon. It looked up at him and made a sound like a bark.

Renick and Lainey skidded to a halt next to Thane. The dragon barked again, then turned and wandered into the cave.

"Go ahead," Thane said. He motioned to Renick and Lainey that they should follow. "I want to hide our tracks." The other two nodded and disappeared into the dark opening.

Thane moved around the area, rubbing out any signs of their passage. He took the time to lay a false trail leading deeper into the mountains. Carefully he backtracked and joined the others in the cave.

Renick had devised a makeshift torch. He, Lainey, and the dragon stood in the small circle of light it afforded.

"We have to go deeper," Thane told them. "As far back as we can."

Lainey cast a worried glance into the darkness. "I'm afraid," she whispered.

Thane laid a hand on her shoulder, and Renick moved to hold her opposite hand. "It'll be okay. We'll keep you safe."

Together they descended into the darkness.

The Dark

Renick winced as Lainey pulled his shirt over his head. She gasped and her fingers fell on her lips.

"Oh, Renick."

He shrugged. "It's not so bad." His face betrayed him as he cringed at the pain.

"Where does it hurt ... the worst?" Lainey asked.

At first he did not know how to respond—every inch of his body hurt. He rolled his shoulders, and a throbbing pain replied. "My shoulder," he answered.

"Being tied up probably aggravated it." She moved to kneel behind him. Her cold hands kneaded his sore shoulder and after a while, the muscles relaxed. "Better?"

Renick nodded.

"Now to see to the rest of you," she said. Starting from the back and working her way across his torso, Lainey cleaned and applied a thick goo to each cut and scrape. Next, she smeared a dark foul-smelling paste on his bruises. When she was done, Renick felt almost normal again.

"Thanks," he said with a tired sigh.

"Here," Lainey said, handing him a waterskin. "Drink as much as you can, and then you need to rest."

After taking a long drink, Renick settled down next to the

fire. He looked across at Lainey; her golden hair glowed softly in the firelight. Her eyes watched the flames, her hands gently petting Plyth, who slept curled up in her lap. Now that she was done fussing over him, Lainey had fallen unusually quiet.

Renick knew he should probably say something. He searched for the right words and at last settled on "It's cold."

She looked up at him and tried to smile. The corners of her mouth twitched a little bit.

"And dark," Renick said.

Lainey closed her eyes. "I know." She started mumbling to herself. Renick thought it sounded like she was saying, "I'm safe. There is air and a way out. I'm safe." Her face looked pale and drawn.

Renick moved around the fire to sit next to Lainey and wrapped his arm around her shoulders. It was how he used to comfort his little sisters when storms raged at night. "Thane'll be back from scouting soon," he told her.

The echo of movement filled the dark air. Renick sat up, drawing his knife. "Who goes there?"

"It's just me." Thane emerged into the small circle of firelight, his hands raised in surrender.

Renick relaxed. Thane held out a bird to Lainey. "I brought you a present—a fine pheasant for a fine lady." Her eyes did not move from the fire. Thane looked over at Renick, who offered to take the bird.

"I'll cook it up for us." They sat in silence while Renick prepared and cooked the bird. Thane carved the bird and handed out strips of the warm meat. Renick fed Plyth, who wiggled happily in Lainey's lap, with a few raw pieces he had saved.

"Can we leave now?" Lainey asked when their meal was done. The pleading in her voice made it tremble.

Thane shook his head. "They're still looking for us. With the way they're circling through the foothills, I can't see a way for us to get out. I'm not sure how long they'll keep it up. It could be days."

Lainey shook her head. "I can't stay here that long."

Renick put his arm around her again.

"It's all right," Thane said. "We'll keep looking. We'll find a way."

"Home." Plyth yawned and stretched out on Lainey's lap.

"Yes, Plyth, we're trying to get home," Lainey said. She gently stroked the ridges on the baby dragon's neck.

Plyth jerked his head back and forth. "Plyth home."

"Where?" Lainey asked as she gazed down at Plyth.

"High rocks," Plyth answered.

"I think he means the mountains," Lainey said. "I think Plyth lives there."

"Poor little guy," Renick said. He reached down and scratched behind Plyth's ear. "He's homesick."

"Home safe," Plyth said.

Thane snorted. "What're we going to do in a dragon's nest? It's probably empty anyway."

Lainey gasped and covered Plyth's ears with her hands. "Thane! What a terrible thing to say. Show some compassion."

It was hard to tell in the dim light, but Renick thought Thane's cheeks might have colored a little. Thane hung his head and grumbled an apology.

"Well, don't you think a mother dragon would choose a safe place to lay her eggs? She would at least find a hidden place to build her nest. You know, somewhere not easy for the hunters to find," Lainey said.

Renick wondered if her insistence that Plyth's home would be safe was in earnest, or if she was that desperate to get out of the cave. Renick turned to Thane. "I don't know. Would we even be able to get into the mountains?"

Thane shrugged. "Possibly. The hunters seem to be focusing on the foothills and the forest around them."

"Maybe they don't expect us to head for the mountains," Lainey offered.

Thane pressed his lips together. "More likely they're laying a trap for us."

Lainey's shoulders sank. "Really?"

In his mind, Renick saw the image of a large white dragon

with blue eyes. He had an impression that she was an old dragon and somehow related to Plyth. His mother's mother, maybe?

"Your grandmother?" Lainey asked. She must have felt the same communication from Plyth.

Plyth wiggled his head. "Granmoder."

"I think Plyth is trying to tell us that his grandmother can help us," Lainey said hopefully.

"It's too dangerous," Thane said.

"What if we go at night?" Lainey pleaded. "Under the cover of darkness and all that." She waved her hand in annoyance.

Thane's brow creased. "I know you're scared, Lainey. But being stuck in this cave is better than being caught by those hunters. Just ask Renick."

Lainey gave Renick a doubtful look. "Renick, what do you think?" Her eyes spoke of fear and hope.

Renick turned to Thane, whose expression was unreadable.

"Home. Near," Plyth urged.

Renick crossed his arms over his chest and considered the two options. The cave was safe for now. The hunters had not ventured into it and the deep darkness would hinder them even if they did. However, Renick and his friends could not stay there forever. The thought of having a full-grown dragon for protection also appealed to him. He wished Thane would make the decision instead of leaving it to him, but one glance confirmed that Thane was waiting for his response. Renick decided it came down to one thing—how long they could stay in the cave.

"How much food do we have?" Renick asked.

Thane closed his eyes. "Not much. But we can hunt for more."

"Any time we leave the cave, we're putting ourselves at risk. We either stay or go." Lainey's breath caught at the end. Renick saw tears sparkling in her eyes.

"All right, then. We leave. Tonight when it's dark, we'll go find Plyth's grandmother," Renick said.

Plyth ran around in a quick little circle and then jumped

into Renick's lap. Lainey clapped her hands and laughed.

Thane's eyebrows and nose scrunched together, but he nodded. "Tonight," he said.

"We're taking you home." Lainey reached out and patted the baby dragon.

The Climb

Renick scanned the blackness of night; his ears strained for any abnormal sound. Off to his left, some wildlife moved through the bush. Holding his breath, he listened even more intently; his ears ached in the silence. After his breath ran out, Renick started breathing quietly, resisting the urge to suck in big gulps of air.

He could not be sure in the darkness, but he did not think there were any hunters up ahead. That would have to be good enough. He crouched down and slunk through the woods back to the opening of the cave where Lainey stood waiting, Plyth in her arms. Her eyes shone in the moonlight.

Thane appeared in the small clearing around the black emptiness of the cave's mouth. "Well?" he asked in a harsh whisper.

Renick shrugged. "I didn't see or hear anything."

Thane harrumphed. "That's not saying much tonight. I can't see my hand in front of my face."

Lainey asked, "Is it safe?"

"There's no way to tell, Lainey," Thane answered. "They might very well be watching us right now."

Lainey's gray eyes turned and darted over the trees around them. "Right now?" she whispered.

"We have to risk it. It's now or never. They either catch us trying to get over the mountain now, or when our food runs out. Personally, I'd rather go now," Renick said.

"I vote now," Lainey agreed.

"Now it is," Thane said.

Thane turned and led the way through the trees toward the mountain. They inched forward, taking small, light steps. The full moon above emerged from behind a cloud and gave off just enough light for Renick to see a few paces in front of him. He kept his eyes on the ground ahead. He could see the back of Lainey's feet as she picked her way along. He watched his feet too, making sure to avoid any stray twigs.

All around him, the night creatures of the forest stirred. With every shaking of a branch or rustling of fallen leaves, Renick stopped and turned his head. He waited, holding his breath until the sound receded. As they drew nearer to the mountainside, the ground began to slope upward. The earth beneath their feet turned from soft to rocky and the trees thinned out. Soon they were in the open. The fickle moonlight faded in and out. They slowed in the darkness and moved more quickly in the light.

Renick noticed that he was falling behind and quickened his pace to catch up with Lainey. When he reached her, she had stopped. Renick looked around for Thane. He was standing just a few paces ahead of them, looking up at a ramp of rocks that led up to the mountain heights.

Thane motioned them to come closer. Renick and Lainey drew together to form a tight circle with Thane.

"As near as I can tell, this slope leads up to some kind of shelf or ledge. If we can reach the top, we should be well hidden from those below," Thane told them.

Lainey looked up at the daunting task. "Isn't there another place to climb? Somewhere less ... mountainy?"

"We don't have time," Thane said.

Renick nodded. "I agree with Thane. Let's climb here and take our chances."

Plyth filled Renick's mind with the image of his

grandmother again. Renick felt an overwhelming sense of longing and the promise of safety. It echoed his own yearning for home.

"Looks like Plyth agrees too," Lainey said, casting her eyes down.

Thane placed a hand on Laincy's shoulder. "We can make it," he told her when she looked up at him. She smiled and set her mouth in a thin line.

"I can do it," she declared.

"All right, then." Renick rubbed his hands together. "Let's get climbing."

Renick started up the mountainside first. The rocks slipped beneath his feet and he had to bend over and use his hands to steady himself. When he found a stable place to stop, he turned to look back over his shoulder.

"Thane, you'd better put Plyth in the pack and take him," Renick called down as loudly as he dared. He saw Thane nod in agreement and turn to Lainey. Renick continued up the slope.

If he had thought their movement through the forest had been slow, he was mistaken. His progress up the slippery slope of the mountain was infinitely more tedious. It felt like for every step he took forward, he slid back two. With some effort, Renick found a method that allowed him to climb more quickly. He walked sideways with a slightly upward slant, using both his hands to steady him. When he reached a portion of especially loose rock, he would turn and start moving in the other direction.

About halfway up, Renick made a turn and glanced below him. He could see Lainey following his lead. She and Thane were quite far behind Renick, so he decided to pause so they could catch up. While he waited, he scanned the sky and the forest below.

A dark figure moved in the shadows under a tree. Renick's heart froze. His breath locked in his chest.

Turning, he tried to get Lainey and Thane's attention, but they were both focused on the arduous task of ascending the mountain. Reaching down, Renick pulled up a handful of rocks and pushed them down toward Lainey. When the pebbles rolled over her hands, Lainey looked up, a question on her face. Renick pointed to the forest and tried to mouth the word "hunter" to her. Fear spread across her face. She turned to Thane, who was waiting behind her. Renick could see them talking in low whispers, but could not hear them.

Thane looked up at Renick and motioned for him to hurry to the top. Turning, Renick started to climb the slope as quickly as he could, not caring about dislodging rocks or making noise. They had been spotted and now they needed to make all haste.

With nothing between him and the hunters below but wide-open space, Renick felt exposed. He resisted the urge to look behind him. It would only slow him down.

Up and up he climbed.

A faint shout sounded from below. Three heartbeats later, an arrow buried its head in the rocks next to him. Renick scrabbled on faster. He chanced a quick look down the slope. Lainey and Thane were still following. Another arrow landed next to his hand. It stuck in the rocks and slid down with the pebbles Renick dislodged as he moved on.

The sky brightened ever so slightly as predawn approached. Soon the hunters would have more light to see and aim by. Renick's shoulder began to ache and his bruises throbbed as he pushed himself to move faster.

Renick caught sight of a ledge jutting out into the loose rocks like a peninsula. Changing his course, he headed straight for the ledge. His hand pressed down on firm rock. With a grunt of effort, Renick pulled himself onto the ledge and stood.

From his new vantage point, Renick could see the hunters massed together near the base of the mountainside. Some of them were trying to follow Thane and Lainey up the slope. Lainey was close to Renick—a few more steps and she would join him. Thane was not far behind.

Renick turned to the mountains; it looked as if the side of

the rock face had fallen away, tumbling down toward the ground. He had been climbing up the landslide. To his left, the range was whole, with plenty of solid ground. Looking around, he tried to find some cover or a place to hide. He saw some large rocks that would probably work. Lainey scrambled up to stand beside him.

"Over there." Renick said, pointing.

Lainey sprinted forward and disappeared behind a tall boulder.

A few moments later, when Renick rounded the corner with Thane on his heels, Lainey was gone.

Breathing Fire

"Lainey," Renick called in a harsh whisper. "Lainey!"

A muffled cry was the only answer. Thane and Renick shared a worried glance and ran around a small outcropping of rocks.

Gunther stood near the ledge holding Lainey's neck in his burly hand. Lainey clawed frantically at the hunter's fingers while her feet swung helpless. "Gotcha," Gunther growled. Lainey tried to turn her head away, gagging.

Thane planted his feet and drew his sword. "Unhand her at once!" he demanded. Plyth poked his head over Thane's shoulder and hissed at the hunter.

Gunther just laughed. He reached down to his belt and drew a long-bladed knife. In one movement Gunther drew Lainey closer to him and turned her to face out towards where Renick and Thane stood. Gunther rested the knife on her neck. "What's that?"

Thane paled.

Renick took a step forward, his hand out as if to placate the angry man. The hunter sneered at him and pressed the knife closer to Lainey. She gasped. Renick could see her jaw tighten to stifle a cry. Her eyes looked up at him, pleading, helpless. Renick wanted to tell her it would be all right, that they would save her. But all he could do was nod.

Lainey's eyes skipped over to Thane's sword and then back to Renick. She blinked and the fear evaporated from her face. Lainey lowered her hands from where they had been clutching at Gunther's sausage fingers; a determined look glinted in her eye.

"I'd put yer sword down, boy, if I were ya." Gunther flashed a smile full of rotting teeth.

Thane lowered his sword and rested the tip in the dirt.

Plyth let out a low wail that warbled and changed pitch. There was a complicated mental undercurrent to the sound. In it, Renick saw the color of Plyth's scales, the image of Plyth's grandmother and another adult dragon. He heard the sound of wind and water dripping into a pool. He tasted salt and some kind of sweet berry. Plyth's dragon song.

Renick's mouth gaped in awe. "So the legend is true," he whispered.

Thane's head tilted toward him slightly, a question on his face. Renick gave a slight shake of his head. "Later."

The sound of Plyth's call trailed off, and with it went the images.

"Quiet," Gunther growled.

Plyth repeated the call. Gunther sheathed his blade and tried to grab the baby dragon, but Thane moved to block him. For an instant, it looked like the hunter would lose his balance. Lainey took advantage of his lack of attention and twisted out of his grasp. Renick reached out and grabbed Lainey's wrist, pulling her behind him. At the same time, Thane brought his sword up and laid it on Gunther's shoulder.

The hunter, using his leather bracer, pushed Thane's sword away. From behind his back, Gunther produced a crossbow. With steady hands, he loaded a bolt and leveled it at Thane's chest. "Go on, boy, see how close ya get."

Plyth called again, the new notes blending with the fading ends of the first one.

"If I were you," Thane said without flinching, "I would leave us alone. Or you might find yourself the main course in a dragon's breakfast." He rolled the hilt of his sword and the blade caught the first light of morning.

Gunther stood his ground. "Whose gonna answer the worm? 'is mother's cut up and burned."

Renick and Lainey's gasps blended together.

"If it were within my power," Thane said, clutching his sword even tighter, "you wouldn't live to see the sun rise."

Gunther opened his mouth, a grin on his face. But the laugh froze in his throat, his eyes fixed on a point in the sky above their heads.

Turning, Renick saw the form of a dragon against the early morning sky. It hovered above them in the air, white scales catching the golden rays of sunrise. The air throbbed with every beat of the massive wings.

A startled, gurgling shout burst out of Gunther. The white dragon dove for the hunter and picked him up in her back talons. Clutching the screaming man, the dragon soared into the air. Gunther's wailing grew more desperate as it faded away. Renick watched as Gunther's form fell from the sky down to the ground. Renick rushed to the edge of the mountain and, scrambling up a pile of rocks, peered over the edge.

Gunther lay in a broken pile surrounded by the other hunters. Some of the hunters who had been climbing the mountain were now trying to scurry down it. The white dragon swept across them, flames pluming from its jaws.

Next to Renick, Thane laughed. "Take that!" he yelled, throwing a fist into the air.

Lainey clapped her hands and Plyth let out a happy squeal.

A group of hunters was trying to load the large crossbow they carried.

"Look out," Renick called, pointing to the danger below.

The white dragon arched her neck and redirected her flight. With a loud roar, she landed on the weapon, causing the hunters to scatter. With a mighty beat of her wings, the dragon lifted the crossbow into the air and smashed it against the rocks. The sound of snapping strings and splintering wood echoed against the walls of the mountain range.

Another roar sent the hunters fleeing into the woods. Renick saw them hover just beyond the line of trees, waiting. A moving shadow caught his attention—he squinted and leaned forward.

"Careful," Thane said, laying a hand on Renick's shoulder.

"Look." Renick pointed down at the trees below.

"What?" Lainey asked.

"There," Renick said. "Do they have another crossbow?"

Thane moved along the ridge a little way, then crouched down and inspected the forest below. "I think so, but it's a smaller one."

"Are they going to ..." Lainey cast a look down at Plyth, who lay nestled in her arms, " ... you know." She hunched her shoulders forward.

Thane shook his head. "Not unless she flies closer."

Just then a hunter stumbled out of the trees as if he had tripped. The dragon, who had been gliding over the trees roaring and breathing fire, circled and dove for the exposed hunter.

Renick stood and cupped his hands around his mouth. "Wait! It's a trap!"

Plyth cried out too—a warning mixed with fear hummed through the air and added an undertone to Renick's words.

The white dragon pulled back, flapping her leathery wings with a mighty effort. The trees at the edge of the forest tossed to and fro under the currents of air, and the grass was flattened. The hunter lying sprawled on the ground raised an arm to block the dust and dirt. It was too late—the white dragon was in range and one of the hunters let loose a bolt.

"No," Lainey gasped.

Renick held his breath, watching as the black bolt flew through the air. The dragon expelled a stream of fire from her powerful jaws. When the flames dissipated, the remaining burned-out husk spiraled out of control, just missing the dragon's right wing.

"Yeah!" Renick cheered, throwing both his hands into the

air.

At the same time, Thane slapped the rock he was leaning on. "That'll show them!"

Lainey let out a breath that puffed out the hair hanging above her eyes.

The white dragon let out a screech of annoyance much like the one Renick's mother used when she found a trail of ants in the kitchen. She dove again, this time breathing fire as she went. The ground around the fallen hunter burst into flames. Yellow flames also lapped at the sky from the canopy of the forest. The dark trees engulfed the dragon as she plunged through them. A moment later, she emerged, a hunter held captive in her front claws. The man was frantically trying to load his crossbow. His attempts were thwarted as the dragon started tossing him from claw to claw as she circled higher and higher.

Then she let him fall.

When the hunter landed in the still-smoldering clearing at the base of the mountain, Renick noticed that the other hunters were gone.

"Cowards," Thane said under his breath.

Spreading her almost-translucent wings, the white dragon angled back toward them. Gracefully, she alighted in front of them. From the ground to her withers, the white dragon stood taller than three horses. She was twice as big as the largest domesticated dragon Renick had ever seen. From square snout to the tip of her tail, she was easily sixty paces long. Renick had to turn his head to see the full extent of her wingspan. A trail of silver spikes started in a cluster between her eyes and arched down along her neck and back, between her wings, and ended with another cluster at the end of her tail. Renick's mouth fell open in appreciation. She was a magnificent dragon.

Plyth leapt out of Lainey's arms and bounded up to his grandmother. He ran circles around her legs, yelping excitedly. Renick felt a sense of coming home, of being with loved ones again. It made him homesick for his own family, chaos and all.

The white dragon lowered her face to Plyth and tenderly

blew on him. Plyth launched a rapid succession of images and feelings. Renick sensed that Plyth's grandmother was responding, but he was not getting any of that side of the conversation.

Renick saw Plyth's mother fall from the sky. Felt the pain and fear the baby dragon experienced as he fell to the forest floor. Renick saw his face, and the faces of Thane and Lainey, and felt the growing trust and friendship of the little dragon.

A growl rumbled from the white dragon's throat. She looked at Renick, sharp, intelligent eyes considering him.

"Humans," she hissed with an undercurrent of distrust and hatred that echoed in Renick's mind.

Lainey let out a small shriek that sounded like a mouse. She clasped her hands to her mouth in an attempt to erase the noise. Thane stood with his hand halfway to his sword and his shoulder tilted back, as if he did not know whether to fight or flee.

She could talk. That same thought circled over and over in Renick's head. She, a dragon, could talk. Plyth was not the only one. He shook his head to recover and looked over at Thane and Lainey, who still stood motionless.

Not knowing what else to do, and clearly being the only one capable of rational behavior at the moment, Renick stepped forward. "I'm Renick. Thank you for rescuing us." He made his best effort at a bow.

The white dragon huffed.

"Trusted," Plyth told his grandmother. She tilted her massive head to the side and sniffed at Renick.

Lainey stepped up beside him and curtsied. "I'm Lainey, madam. I extend my gratitude to you for your service."

"Kind," Plyth hummed.

Thane cleared his throat and bowed quickly. "Thane, milady. My thanks for aiding my friends when I couldn't."

Plyth tossed his head. "Brave."

Renick thought this made the white dragon laugh. She made a staccato gurgling sound and wiggled her head back and forth.

"Young humans," she said. Leaning back, she sat on her hind legs and rose to her full height, spread her wings, and looked down at them. "I am Wrytha Whitewing of the Dragon Kind, member of the Seventh Circle. And you are trespassing on our lands." She let out a long bugle sound and bared her teeth.

Surprised, Renick found himself taking a few steps backwards. A flurry of questions filled his mind and leapt to his lips—thankfully he was too stunned to utter them. Instead, he tried to remember the etiquette his mother had so desperately wanted to teach him and his siblings. He wished now that he had paid just a little more attention. "We apologize. We didn't know this land was yours. We're lost and trying to find our way out of the forest and back to our people."

Wrytha laughed. This time Renick not only heard the sound, but the mirth also echoed in his mind. She lowered herself to the ground. It made her seem less intimidating.

"Fear not, little ones, I will not eat you—today." Her eyes smiled down at them. "You helped my grandson?"

Renick nodded. "His wing was broken. Lainey and I set the bone. The bandages will need to be removed eventually."

A wave of gratitude washed over him. "Our young are precious to us. Your deeds have saved you from an awful fate."

She turned and Renick took the opportunity to look at Thane and Lainey again. Lainey mouthed the words, "She can talk." Renick nodded excitedly in response.

Wrytha angled her head around to look at them. Renick could have sworn she had a questioning look on her face. "Come, Renick-Trusted, Lainey-Kind, and Thane-Brave. We must take cover before the hunters find their courage and come after us."

Dragon's Nest

Renick looked up at Wrytha, who stood at the peak of a sharp incline, waiting for them. Plyth sat next to her, his body shaking as he wagged his tail back and forth. Renick turned his attention back to climbing up to the two dragons.

"They can talk," he said to himself with a shake of his head. His father's favorite story came to mind, the one Renick had always begged to be told at bedtime as a child, the one he thought of every time he spent a long night with a sick dragon or hatchling. The one he dreamed about. Renick was confronted with the impossible, two dragons that could speak—that could communicate with him. A chill of excitement ran up his skin.

"Renick," Lainey said breathlessly beside him, "it's just so amazing, isn't it?"

He nodded. "Talking dragons."

"I never would've thought in a million years. I mean, I used to have a cat. Well, really, my cousins had a cat—I just played with her a lot. And I'd talk to her and imagine that she'd talk back. But I never really expected her to respond. I think if I'd ever had a pet dragon, I'd have done the same." She chattered on, rambling in her excitement.

A rock landed between the two of them. Lainey stopped

talking and they both looked down the slope to where Thane was. He placed a finger to his lips and then pointed up above them. Renick followed the line of Thane's finger and saw Wrytha watching them. He suddenly felt very uneasy.

"Would you two watch it? Besides it's not that earth shattering—Plyth can talk so someone must've taught him."

"So you said your cousins had a cat. Where was that?" Renick asked, trying to sound casual.

"Morelindar. A few years ago. I think it died, actually." She smiled at him sadly and then went back to concentrating on the climb.

Renick paused, resting his sore shoulder and letting his thoughts wander. Soon, Thane passed him too. As Renick watched Thane scramble up the rocks, he thought of how his father would have loved to meet Wrytha and Plyth and would probably know how to react to them. His father knew more of the dragon lore—which apparently was more than just myth.

Lainey waved to Renick from the top of the rise, and when she had his attention, she motioned him to join them. Renick started climbing again as he searched his mind for any stories or lore that spoke of how to be polite to a dragon. But his memory failed him.

By the time he reached the top of the climb, Wrytha had already moved ahead. She now stood next to the opening of a shallow cave at the bottom of a dip in the mountain. The others were making their way toward her. Renick looked up, shielding his eyes from the sun. All he could see was an endless expanse of blue sky. Not even a wisp of a cloud marred the brilliant blue. It was so peaceful, so quiet.

He skidded down the slope to join his friends. Wrytha tossed her head in the direction of the cave. Lainey wrung her hands nervously, so Renick went in first. There was more light in the cave than he had suspected from looking in. The depression in the rock was just big enough for a dragon of Wrytha's size to lie comfortably and have room to turn around. The floor was mostly occupied by a pile of straw and soft leaves.

"It's not bad, Lainey. Very open." Renick motioned to her.

She dropped her hands to her sides and bit her lip. Then, with a confident toss of her head, she marched into the cave. Taking a deep breath, she looked around. "You're right." She smiled. "Not bad at all."

"Cozy," Thane said with a straight face.

Renick was confused at first, but then Lainey started to laugh. She wrapped her arms around her stomach and shook with laughter. Thane licked his lips and tried to act aloof, but Renick could see the corner of the older boy's mouth twitching.

Finding a place to sit, Renick lowered himself to the ground and leaned his head against the wall of the cave. Lainey knelt beside him.

"How are you?" Her brow and lips pinched in a concerned expression.

"Fine." He tried to wave her away.

Wrytha's head appeared next to Lainey. She jumped a little when the dragon sniffed at Renick's hair.

"You are injured, Renick-Trusted." Wrytha observed.

Renick nodded. The dragon seemed to study him for a moment.

"Help?" Plyth asked.

Wrytha bobbed her head. "All right, little one." She bent her head low and placed her snout on Renick's forehead. Her warm breath seemed to spread through Renick's entire body. He felt a small pop in his shoulder and the muscles around it relaxed. All the stiff pain and tightness melted away and he was left feeling calm and whole.

"How did you do that?" Renick asked in wonder, rolling his shoulder and then lifting his shirt in search of bruises. His skin was clean—not a scrape or a bruise remained.

"Magic," Lainey said, her eyes wide, her fingers reaching toward Renick.

Wrytha chuckled, but Renick felt a questioning undertone in his mind. The dragon turned to Lainey and then Thane, blowing her hot breath on them as well. Renick could see them each slump down in relief after her touch.

Last, she turned to Plyth.

"Remove the bandage," she instructed Lainey.

Lainey's slim fingers worked at the knots holding the splint in place and then unwrapped Plyth's broken wing. Wrytha watched her work.

"You have done well, Lainey-Kind—for a human." Wrytha healed Plyth with the same hot breath. When she was done, he flapped the wing experimentally and then barked with happy laughter.

"Fly!" he crooned.

"Not now, little one," Wrytha told him. "It is not safe." She turned to face Renick, Thane, and Lainey. "Wait here—you will be well hidden. I will be back before nightfall." The white dragon withdrew her head from the cave, spread her wings, and took flight.

Lainey bent to inspect Plyth's wing. "Amazing," she said, and her eyes got a faraway look in them. "If only ..." She shook her head and did not finish the thought.

"Where do you think she went?" Thane asked.

Renick shrugged. "Maybe she's checking on the hunters. They could've regrouped by now."

Thane watched Wrytha's form fade away. He crossed his arms. "I don't know. She seems ..."

"Skeptical," Lainey offered.

"Exactly."

Renick looked between the two of them. "Maybe she's never met a human who can talk."

Thane arched an eyebrow at him. His expression caused a smile to spread across Lainey's face, which she quickly hid.

"What?" Renick held his hands up in surrender.

"And where do you suggest she would've met a human who *couldn't* talk?" Thane said in a condescending tone.

"I ... don't know."

"I have a great-uncle once removed who lives near a colony of mutes." There was mirth dancing behind Lainey's eyes. "Maybe she's been there." Her lips moved to contain a giggle, but another smile escaped.

Renick could not resist it any longer. He laughed long and hard. After the past few days, it felt good. The remaining tension eased from his body and he suddenly felt tired.

"Perhaps we should rest," Renick offered.

Thane nodded. "Finally, a rational suggestion." He found a spot at the back of the cave and made himself comfortable.

"Renick," Lainey said as she nestled into the soft nest with Plyth cuddled under her chin, "tell us another dragon story."

He nodded and started the story that had been on his mind ever since he heard Plyth speak. "A long time ago, in a village near the sea, there lived a young boy named Ponti. His father was a fisherman and very poor. To help his family survive, Ponti would often walk the beaches and climb the cliffs in search of things he could sell for a coin or two."

Lainey leaned back and closed her eyes. Renick lowered his voice just a little and noticed that in response, Thane stopped digging in the dirt with his knife.

"One day, Ponti found a dragon's nest. It looked as if the nest's owner had long since abandoned it. And so, assuming that anything left behind wasn't wanted, he searched the nest. Buried in the far corner, he found a very rare seashell. The money he could get for it would feed his family well for a month. With an empty stomach growling in anticipation, Ponti put the shell under his shirt and returned home."

Plyth snorted in his sleep and a little puff of smoke wafted up from his nostrils. Lainey lazily patted his head. Renick lay down and stared at the cave's ceiling.

"Some time later, when the money from the shell was spent and his stomach once more empty, Ponti climbed to the dragon's nest again. This time he found the nest occupied by a beautiful blue dragon. She sat atop three eggs." Renick paused and started drumming his fingers on his stomach. When he resumed speaking, he matched the dictation to their beat. It was something his father often did while narrating.

"The dragon turned to him and asked, 'Are you the boy who took my shell?'

"Ponti suddenly felt afraid. He stammered out an apology, explaining that he hadn't known she still lived there. The dragon just laughed at him and said, 'No apologies are necessary. It sounds as if your need was greater than mine. Tell me, would you like another seashell?' Ponti eagerly nodded his head. 'Then watch my eggs for me tonight. Stay with them and keep them warm. And when I return in the morning, I will bring you another shell,' the dragon offered. Ponti quickly agreed. So she took flight, leaving Ponti to tend to her unhatched. Ponti stayed in the cave all night, tending a fire and keeping the eggs warm."

Lainey's breathing had fallen into a regular rhythm. Renick moved his head so he could see Thane. The older boy was watching him, so Renick continued. "In the morning, the dragon did not return. Ponti stood looking out to sea, waiting. At midday, he climbed down from the nest and returned home. There he gathered up some blankets, a fishing rod, and what few things his mother could spare and returned to the nest. For four days and three more nights, Ponti tended the dragon's eggs."

Renick stopped, his attention drawn away by a shadow that fell over the cave entrance.

"Did she ever come back?" Thane asked.

"Yes. And she rewarded the boy with a shell for each night that he cared for her young. He used the money to buy his father a better fishing boat, and the family never went hungry again. But more than that, he and the dragon became friends. They taught and helped each other for the rest of their days."

"An interesting story," Wrytha said, her head appearing around the edge of the cave. "Where did you hear it?"

"It's a fable my father used to tell to me," Renick said.

"A fable?"

"Well, it couldn't be true—the dragon talks." Renick laughed at himself. "A silly thing to say to a dragon that can speak."

Wrytha was quiet for a time. Her eyes stayed locked on Renick as if she were trying to see inside him, to hear his thoughts—as if she could peel away his skin and see his soul.

"Come," she said. Lainey and Plyth stirred at her words. "The others wish to meet you."

Dragon City

Renick tilted his head back to look at the cave where Wrytha had led them. The black opening rose above him and almost swallowed the sky. Two dragon statues, carved out of the stone that formed the sides of the opening, sat as silent sentinels. Their cold eyes stared down at him as if waiting for him to speak.

A hand touched Renick's arm.

"What is it?" Lainey asked.

"Nothing." He shrugged. "Just something I almost remember."

Wrytha and the others were waiting for them just outside the cave.

"Go ahead. You three first." Wrytha's voice remained calm, but there was something under the surface, something she did not want them to know.

Squinting at her, Renick tried to feel her projected thoughts the way he did with Plyth. Faint images and thoughts floated just out of his reach. He tried to concentrate harder.

Secret. Wrytha's voice hissed in his mind. *Hidden. Secret.*

Curious, Renick wondered what she could be hiding from them. He tried to focus on an image that kept resurfacing. When he could almost see it, a burning sensation erupted behind his eyes. Renick pinched the bridge of his nose. The pain caused him to lose focus.

Do not tread where you are not wanted. Wrytha turned and looked at him. Renick stood motionless, hardly breathing under the scrutiny of the angered dragon. She puffed a small cloud of smoke through her nostrils and shook her head.

"Go on," Wrytha urged, no hint of anger or frustration in her voice. Without hesitation, Renick followed behind Thane and Lainey as they marched into the dark cavern.

The light from the sun disappeared and for a moment they were walking in darkness. Then a red-gold glow illuminated the passageway. Renick moved toward the colored light, stumbling a little along the way.

Four large dragons surrounded them. They moved in from the dim corners of the chamber, seeming to come from the walls themselves. Lainey gasped and clutched at Thane's arm. Feeling unsure, Renick turned and walked backwards until he stood in a tight circle with his friends.

Renick watched the massive dragons draw closer. There were two greens, one red, and a blue. Their scales were bright, brilliant colors like none he had ever seen. The glow, which came from four orbs mounted on the cavern walls, made the dragons sparkle and gleam. Their eyes shone with dark and foreboding intelligence.

The air seemed to buzz around him. A barrage of images and emotions assaulted his mind. Renick turned his head as if he could stem the flow. The confusion made his temples throb with pain.

"They're talking to each other," Renick whispered.

One of the dragons hissed at him. "Silence." The word echoed in Renick's mind.

"You ..." Lainey did not have a chance to finish her sentence.

"Silence," the dragon repeated.

The two dragons on Renick's left shifted and formed a wall with the other two. Together the four massive dragons—all the same size or bigger than Wrytha—stepped forward. Renick instinctively drew back. The dragons continued to move forward, driving Renick and the others.

"What's going on?" Lainey whispered.

One of the dragons let out a jet of hot air. Lainey yelped and spun around, trying to cover her back with her hands. The dragons shifted their weight impatiently.

In the chaos that echoed in Renick's skull, he thought he could hear a word, or at least understand one cluster of thought. *Move,* it seemed to say. He reached down and took Lainey's hand and drew her forward with him.

The dragons ushered them on.

They were being herded through a series of tunnels bored deep into the mountain. In some places, the tunnels were open on one side. Renick could see out into a giant chamber. Sunlight filtered down from above and dragons flew back and forth in the cool air. He wondered if the mountain was hollow. Or maybe the chamber was actually a gap between the mountains. Either way, Renick was grateful for the fresh air that flowed through the tunnels. At points on their march where the sunlight did not reach them, there were more glowing orbs attached to the walls. Renick studied them as they passed. The surface looked like glass, but rippled like water. Deep inside, a small ring of flame churned and spun, giving off the odd light.

"Dragon lanterns," Renick said under his breath.

"What?" Lainey asked, her voice trembling.

He pointed to the orbs. "They remind me of the dragon lanterns my father makes for special occasions."

One of their captors snapped his jaws at them. Renick and Lainey turned and continued their march in silence. Soon the dragons stopped in front of an opening in the tunnel. Here there was no sunlight. Instead, two of the glowing orbs stood on either side of the black archway. The dragons pushed Renick and the others into the darkness.

Renick found himself standing in the middle of a small, hollowed-out chamber. It was roughly the size of a cottage and seemed large enough to hold two or three wild dragons. A single orb glowed at the back of the chamber, giving off just enough light to see by.

The blue and one of the green dragons left. Renick watched as the remaining two dragons turned their backs and filled the opening of the chamber with their massive bodies.

"They're leaving us here?" Lainey cried. She was breathing very quickly and rubbing her hands together. "They can't leave us here. There isn't enough air."

Thane walked over and wrapped his arms around her. Lainey sobbed into his shoulder.

"It'll be okay," Renick said, patting her on the back.

"What else can we do?" Thane asked, his eyebrows pinched together.

Renick shrugged. "I don't know. With my sisters, I just told them everything would be fine and waited for the crying to stop."

"Do you think they'd help?" Thane motioned toward the guard dragons with his chin.

Renick approached the dragons, watching their backs apprehensively. "Excuse me," he said, trying to sound confident. "My friend is afraid of small spaces. Could you help her?"

To Renick's surprise, one of the dragons turned around and considered him with black eyes.

"Very well," a deep male voice said.

"Hear that, Lainey? Help is coming," Thane said to Lainey's hair.

She just whimpered and dug her head deeper into his shoulder. Renick wanted to offer more support to his friend, but his head was pounding with the constant jumble of images and thoughts from the two guard dragons, who apparently were in the middle of a heated debate. Something about compassion versus preservation. He could not understand all of it.

"You okay?" Thane asked.

Renick shook his head. "They're talking. It's like trying to listen to a conversation through a door."

Thane's face turned from concerned to skeptical. Renick just shrugged it away.

A short time later, the two dragons moved aside when a third entered. The dragon was small compared to the others they had seen. It had gray scales flecked with red and it moved very slowly. It put its head down next to Lainey, who was still wrapped in Thane's arms.

After smelling and watching her for a moment, the dragon breathed on her. "Sleep," an old female voice said. Lainey slumped in Thane's arms. Renick pulled off his cloak and balled it up for a make-shift pillow, and Thane lowered Lainey to rest her head on it.

"She will sleep now," the dragon said and turned to leave.

"Wait. What about when she wakes up?" Renick asked.

The dragon looked back at him. "Call for me again."

Once the silver dragon left the cell, the two guard dragons took their places again.

Thane stepped up to them. "Why are we being held here? What's going on?"

The dragons did not reply.

"I demand to know why we're being held against our will. I demand to speak to the per ... dragon in charge!" Thane yelled, his voice echoing a little, which added to the force.

Finally the green dragon turned around and looked at him. "Silence. You will know tomorrow."

"That's not good enough," Thane said. "We have a right to know now."

"Humans have no rights here."

Thane's jaw set in a firm line, but he did not argue any further. "Pointless," he mumbled.

"Maybe we should just rest," Renick said. He looked down at Lainey lying peacefully on the ground.

Instead of responding, Thane remained in his defiant stance, arms crossed, staring at the backs of the two dragons.

Renick gave up and settled down as best he could on the cold stone floor. He fell asleep looking at the wall of the chamber, missing the blue sky of his home.

I Trust Them

Plyth did not understand.

"Why friends taken?" Plyth wanted to know. Grandmother would not say. Would not stop to listen.

He felt afraid and lonely, very lonely. Home was not supposed to feel this way. Home was supposed to be safe. Supposed to be happy. He needed his friends.

"Want to see friends," Plyth said, but Grandmother just kept walking. He missed Kind, Brave, and Trusted. He wanted Kind to pat him on the head and sing to him. Trusted could make him feel better, make him feel not lonely. And Brave would protect them all. But friends gone.

Were they okay? Plyth let out a plaintive cry.

Grandmother stopped and looked back. "Calm yourself, Plyth. It will be all right. You are home now. I will care for you."

"Friends, where friends?" He smelled the air. But he could not smell Kind or Trusted. Not even Brave's strong smell. Plyth ran in a circle. He was really scared.

Grandmother blew hot air on him again. Calm touched him on the outside, but did not go inside. She spoke to him in his head, *Calm. Peace. Home. Safety.*

They were back at the nest. It felt empty without his friends there. Plyth found spot where Kind had slept and snuggled in.

"But not home for friends. Where friends?" he asked again.

"It is hard to explain. They are human, like the hunters. They cannot be trusted. They are the enemy," Grandmother said.

"Not hunters. Friends," Plyth said firmly. "Friends!"

She wrapped her body around him, holding him close. "I know. I know they are your friends. But they are not all the dragons' friends. Try to understand. For now they are safe. They are being held captive, but they are safe." She licked him. Licked his head and his scales. *Home. Safe. All is well.*

"Safe now? After now? Still safe?" Plyth could feel his heart beat fast. What would happen to his friends?

Uncle Derth came to the nest. "Welcome home, young one," he said. *Home. Joy. Together.*

Plyth wriggled from Grandmother's grasp. "Friends! Want to see friends. Not hunters!"

"Settle down. It is all right. No one has harmed your friends," Uncle Derth said. More calm, but still did not go inside. Plyth ran in a circle. His uncle and grandmother just watched. They were concerned. He had to settle down or they would not listen.

He sat. Breathed in. Breathed out. Slow. Calm.

"They friends, not hunters," Plyth told Uncle Derth. This time he was not afraid. He was truthful.

Uncle Derth looked at Grandmother. They said things to each other. Kept it hidden from Plyth. Uncle Derth looked back at him. "Plyth ..." he started.

"I trust them!" Plyth said. He felt all the truth and trust and friendship he could. *Trust friends.*

The other two were quiet. After a long time, Uncle Derth dipped his head and looked in Plyth's eyes. "Very well," he said. "Let us go and meet these friends of yours."

Prisoners of War

When Renick woke, he saw Lainey sitting up. Her arms were wrapped around her legs and she was rocking back and forth. Thane sat nearby, talking to her quietly. Renick cast a glance at the guard dragons. He could not feel them talking anymore and the pain in his head had receded.

Renick turned back to Lainey. "How are you?" he asked.

Lainey smiled at him. "I'm fine." The sound of her raw voice made Renick's throat hurt.

The corridor outside their cell filled with the sound of yelping. Plyth's head appeared between the legs of one of the guard dragons, who growled in annoyance. The baby dragon pushed his way into the cave and leapt into Lainey's arms.

"Friends!" Plyth exclaimed.

"It's good to see you too." Lainey giggled, some of the worry melting away from her face.

The two guard dragons made a lot of noise as they shuffled aside to admit Wrytha into the cell. Renick had to move back a little to give her room. "Greetings, Renick-Trusted, Lainey-Kind, and Thane-Brave."

"And why should we greet you? After what you did to us?" Thane snapped at her.

"Thane," Lainey admonished him. Thane stood his ground

and Renick silently hoped he would not have to choose sides in an argument between the two of them. His thoughts and feelings were far too conflicted at the moment.

Wrytha lowered her head almost to the ground; her eyes were full of sorrow. "No, Lainey-Kind, Thane-Brave has a right to be angry with me. You expected to find safety with me. Instead, I played a role in your imprisonment. I apologize, but I am bound by the laws of my kind."

"The Code of the Dragon Kind?" The words escaped Renick's mouth before he realized it. Wrytha's words sparked something—a legend so old his uncle had only known bits and pieces of it. Renick had only heard the tale once or twice, and so a stray phrase here and there was all his weary mind could produce.

"You know of it, Renick-Trusted?" Wrytha asked.

Renick shrugged. "Not really—it's something I heard my uncle say once. I don't know anything more about it."

"I see." She turned and looked back into the hall outside their cell. "I have brought someone to meet you."

"Who is he? The executioner?" Thane's voice dripped with malice.

"No, Thane-Brave. He is someone I hope can help," Wrytha answered. She shifted her weight from side to side as if uncomfortable.

"I think we've had enough of your help already," Thane said.

Lainey jumped up, cradling Plyth in her arms. "Thane Shaytorrin!" Every inch of Lainey's posture spoke of her displeasure. The muscles in Thane's jaw and arms tensed.

Renick went and stood next to Thane, his back facing Wrytha. "We don't have to trust them. Just listen to them, Thane—it's our only option."

Thane's eyes darted over to look at him. Without a word, he spun and marched to the back of the cave. He took up a position leaning against a portion of the wall that was shrouded in darkness.

After watching him for a moment, Renick turned to

Wrytha. "Sorry. This is all a little shocking to us." Renick rubbed the back of his neck with one hand.

"It is all right. I understand his suspicion, Renick-Trusted," the white dragon responded.

"Why do you call him that?" Lainey asked.

"Renick-Trusted? It is his dragon name," Wrytha said.

"Dragon what?" Lainey's brow scrunched together.

"Dragon name. It is a tradition from the old days. Our kind, especially our young, have the ability to see to the core of a person. Plyth has named you three thus—Thane-Brave, Lainey-Kind, and Renick-Trusted." Wrytha bowed her head to each of them in turn.

Lainey's cheeks colored. She looked down at the baby dragon. "I'm honored you think of me as kind."

Renick felt an immense weight settle over his chest. Trusted. What a name to live up to. And at the same time, he wondered if Wrytha saw the same in him. If he was trusted, why were they being held here?

"This is Derth Wisescales. He is a member of the Second Circle," Wrytha said.

Her words drew Renick back to the task at hand. Another dragon entered the small cave. He was half again as tall as Wrytha, with scales a shade of blue so dark it was almost black. A cluster of black spikes erupted on the crown of the dragon's head and traced the outline of his large ears. His black wings and claws blended into the shadows.

"He is here to ask you some questions," Wrytha finished.

Thane stood and stepped just into the light. "We won't answer any questions until you tell us why we're being held."

Derth bared his teeth and hissed. "You are not in a position to make demands, human." He took a few deep breaths and then added in a calmer tone. "Answer my questions satisfactorily and I will answer yours in turn."

Thane did not back down.

"Thane," Lainey said softly, "it's a fair exchange."

After a moment, Thane nodded curtly, but he did not relax his posture.

"How did you come to be in the forest?" Derth asked.

Renick knew it was up to him to answer. "We were all traveling to Trevinni in a flyer when—"

"A flyer?" Wrytha interjected.

"It's ..." Renick was not sure how to describe it. When he pictured it in his mind, Wrytha and Derth huffed.

"One of your enslavement devices," Derth said.

"Enslavement devices?" Renick asked. One of the stories his father told had a dragon slavemaster. For the first time, Renick realized what that meant.

"Do you always do that?" Thane cut in. "Read our thoughts without asking?"

"We do not invade your thoughts; we simply overhear what you direct at us," Derth explained.

Renick shook his head. "Amazing."

"What is amazing, Renick-Trusted?" Wrytha asked.

"You can talk," Renick said. "And hear our thoughts. And we can hear your thoughts."

"You were unaware that our kind could talk?" Derth said. Renick felt an odd sense of confusion and curiosity from the old dragon.

Renick shrugged. "Plyth was the first dragon to talk to me."

"What about the old histories? Do they not speak of talking dragons?" Wrytha said.

"Other than the stories Renick has told us, no," Lainey offered. She had seated herself once again and was gently scratching Plyth under his chin.

"It would appear," Derth said with a low growl, "that the knowledge of our kind has passed from human history."

"Not entirely. Remember Renick-Trusted's stories." Wrytha swung her head until it was very near Renick's head.

"Where did you learn these stories, Renick-Trusted?" Derth asked.

"From my father." Renick swallowed before continuing. "But until I met you, I thought they weren't true."

"Interesting," Derth mused.

A small part of the river of questions Renick had been

holding in suddenly came out in a rush. "They're true though, aren't they? Have dragons always been able to talk? Do all dragons talk?"

"Silence. I will answer your questions the best I can when I am finished." Derth turned his attention to Thane. "You are angry with us. Why?"

Thane remained frozen in place for a moment. "We've done nothing to earn our imprisonment. I want to know why we're here."

"Fair enough," Derth said. "I will answer this one question for you. And then no more until I am satisfied. Agreed?"

Renick watched Thane, anxious for his response. He was just as eager for answers as Thane, but Renick also wanted to learn more about these dragons that seemed to walk right out of legend.

"Agreed," Thane announced as he sat and leaned against the wall of the cave. The older boy almost seemed relaxed, but Renick noticed Thane's hand resting on the hilt of his sword.

"You are prisoners of war," Derth told them.

"What!" Thane sat up, his hand gripping his sword, ready to draw it out.

"War?" Lainey sounded confused.

Renick remembered something else his uncle had said in a conversation with his father long ago. Something about the great dragon war never really being over, even though there were none left to fight it.

"Enough." Derth snapped his jaws, making Renick jump. "I will tell you more if I find I can trust you. Back to my first question—how did you come to be in the forest?"

"Something hit the dragon and tore the sails of the flyer. We crashed. We're lost and trying to find our way to Trevinni," Renick replied.

"Were there others traveling with you?" Wrytha asked.

"Yes," Renick said.

"Where are they?" Derth seemed suspicious.

"We don't know," Lainey said sadly. She looked down at the floor of their cell. Her hands started to shake again.

Wrytha and Derth lowered their heads in what Renick thought might be sympathy.

"My great-nephew tells me you bound his broken wing. Why?" Derth asked, looking first at Lainey and then at Renick.

"He was hurt and alone," Lainey said. She looked up and met Derth's gaze. "That's reason enough for me."

"Same here," Renick said.

"And you saved him from the hunters?" Wrytha asked.

"Yes, you could have surrendered to them. They could have taken you home," Derth added.

"I hadn't thought of that," Renick admitted. "We knew they were hunting dragons. I was sure they killed Plyth's mother. I wouldn't let them get him, too."

Derth was silent for a long time while he studied Renick. The dragon's dark eyes stared at him as if daring him to give away a secret.

"Are you satisfied?" Wrytha asked Derth.

"I am ... curious. I never thought in all my days ..." Derth did not finish his thought; instead, he offered to answer their questions.

"What war?" Thane said before Renick could decide which of his own questions to ask first.

"The great war, the one we have been fighting since before your kind enslaved ours," Derth said. A rumble emanated from his throat and steam hissed out of his jaws, leaking from between his razor-sharp teeth. "Before the lesser dragons fell silent."

"You mean, our dragons—the domestic ones—could be like you?" Two emotions raged inside Renick as he waited for Derth to answer. On one hand, that would be amazing to be able to talk to all dragons. On the other hand, if they were like *these* dragons, then "enslavement" was a good term for how his kind treated them. It made Renick sick to his stomach to think of the dragons being enslaved.

Derth and Wrytha tilted their heads toward Renick. Their feelings of curiosity and amazement broke over him and the pain in his head flared back to life.

"No," Derth said slowly as if he were distracted. "To prevent the knowledge and magic of dragons from being misused by their taskmasters, the ancestors of the enslaved dragons did not pass on any knowledge to their offspring. Those dragons are forever mute and dumb."

Renick felt only a little relieved and more than a little disappointed. "Is that why our ancestors enslaved your race?" he asked. "To use your magic?"

"Yes," Derth and Wrytha answered together.

"Can't the mute dragons be taught to speak?" Renick wondered.

"No." Derth growled. The sound echoed off the walls of their cell. "Enough. No more questions." He turned and left, strode between the two guard dragons almost before they could move aside.

"Touchy subject?" Thane asked.

Wrytha shook her head. "You cannot imagine." She beckoned to Plyth and together they left.

"Wait," Thane called after them. "What's going to happen to us?"

"You will be tried tomorrow. The Inner Circle will decide your fate," Wrytha told them as she disappeared behind the two guard dragons.

Thane stepped close to Renick and said in a low voice, "I don't like this."

"There is not much we can do," Lainey said. "We're trapped." Her voice caught a little.

"We can escape," Thane said.

"How?" Renick asked. "Do you think your sword will do any good against them?" He waved his hands at the guards. "The best thing to do is wait until tomorrow."

Thane shook his head. "I still don't like it."

Dragon Court

It had been a long and sleepless night for Renick. He rubbed at a knot in his neck as he followed behind Derth. Renick and the others were being taken to the dragon hall to appear before the Inner Circle for their trial. He had spent his wakeful night searching his memory for anything that could help them. He had found only one thing—a brief mention of a man who had committed a crime against a dragon. The man was punished according to the dragons' laws and imprisoned for life.

Renick had felt he should not share this story with Thane or Lainey.

The narrow tunnel they were walking through opened into a large chamber. The walls of the chamber were covered with intertwining grooves, like ripples on the water during a rainstorm. Inset in the circles were stones of every color that glowed from an inner light. The cave wall looked like a field of stars on a clear winter night. Renick craned his neck to see every inch of the elaborate design.

"There is a stone for each of the Dragon Kind, the wise dragons, you might call them. The circles represent where we stand in our society," Derth said. Renick turned to see the dark-blue dragon watching him.

"It's beautiful," Lainey said, breathlessly.

"There was a time when this entire cavern was bright as day for the number of dragon stones. Now it grows dim as our kind diminishes." Derth hung his head.

Renick turned back to the beauty of the dragon hall and tried to imagine it filled with glowing gems. His chest tightened with regret at the loss of such a wonderful sight and what it reflected about the Dragon Kind. "I'm sorry," Renick said in a low whisper.

Without warning, a cluster of images and emotions struck Renick's mind. He stumbled backwards, his head on fire with pain. "Please stop," he pleaded. He felt Thane supporting his shoulder and Lainey's warm hand slip into his.

Derth seemed troubled by Renick's reaction, he withdrew his thoughts and Renick's mind quieted in response.

"Here." Lainey pressed something into Renick's hand.

He straightened to stand on his own and looked down at the clump of dried leaves resting in his palm.

"Chew on them—it'll dull the pain a little." Lainey smiled at him.

Renick placed the leaves in his mouth. They tasted bitter. He swallowed some of the juices and the relief was enough to make the terrible taste worth it. "Thanks," he said.

"Come. They are waiting for us." Derth led them along a narrow walkway that circled the chamber.

Casting a glance over the edge, Renick was met with only darkness. At one narrow end of the oblong cavern, a portion of the walkway widened out over the black abyss, creating a sort of platform.

Derth halted. "I will be serving as your advocate. Do not speak unless I tell you to." The dragon waited for each of them to nod in acknowledgement before he stepped onto the platform.

The cavern began to fill with light. Renick looked up to see a shaft leading to the sky above. The little patch of blue grew steadily brighter as somewhere out of sight, the sun started to rise. The growing light flooded into the cavern, revealing its interior. In the center of the chamber, like islands in a sea of night, stood giant stone pedestals. They were arranged in three circles, each inside the other, and rose like steps leading up to the ceiling. Renick noticed that on the wall behind the pedestals, a matching array of circles shone in the early morning sunlight. For each pedestal there was a stone, and on each sat a dragon of answering color.

In the second circle, one of the pedestals stood empty. Renick wondered if it was Derth's place.

Sunshine bathed the walls of the cavern, causing the dragon stones to flash brightly. Renick could now see that there were alcoves, like balconies, high above their heads. Even more dragons, heads down toward him and his friends, filled these balconies. All around him, the air hummed with a sense of anticipation. They were waiting.

Renick felt a shiver run up his spine.

A rumble echoed through the cavern as the dragons gathered there joined together in a single-note chorus. Renick held his breath. The vibrations of the sound penetrated his bones and thrummed through his body. His breath caught in his throat when he felt the emotional undercurrent to the song. Abruptly the dragons' jaws snapped shut, but the echo of their chorus remained, lingering in the cold air of the cavern.

In the silence that followed, Renick noticed the ache returning to his neck and was grateful for the bitter herbs still held between his teeth. He watched the gathered dragons closely. They were turning to look at each other, shifting their stance, groaning and tossing their heads. Then he felt it—a sense of worry and danger. It seemed to pulse through the empty space of the dragon hall, a constant tide of emotion. With the pain in his head dulled by Lainey's herbs, Renick was able to concentrate on the feelings coming from the dragons. Soon they were joined by images and impressions that flew by so fast that he could not keep up with them.

As Renick continued to focus, some of the jumbled thoughts started to form into words in his mind. He could almost hear the conversation.

"Hunters?" someone seemed to say.

"Running. Near south end of forest," a dragon replied.

"Not safe yet," many agreed.

"Keep watching, keep chasing." This seemed to be a decision or an order. Renick could not tell which.

The conversation about the hunters continued for a short while. Renick saw the face of Horrin a few times. One of those image showed him whole, without the scars and missing eye. Renick balked at how much ambition Horrin's past eyes held, contrasted with the anger he had seen.

"The fallen?" The question had a deeply sad undertone to it. Renick's chest tightened.

The images of five dragons flashed in Renick's mind. He recognized one of them, a silvery gray dragon—Plyth's mother.

"Mythaari." Derth's voice echoed in Renick's head.

"Honor. A moment of silence."

Every sound in the chamber stopped. Renick's own breathing slowed until he could not hear it. Not a dragon moved. Renick bowed his head, thinking of Mythaari and the dragon from the flyer.

One of the dragons gave a long, low bugle that ended with a slight catch. The time to mourn was over. Looking up, Renick saw Derth watching him.

The council of dragons moved on to the next topic at hand.

"The humans." He heard this over and over in his head. Some of the whisperings started to take on a personality of their own, and Renick thought he could identify which dragon was speaking.

Renick remembered a time not too long ago when his parents were discussing where they should send him for an apprenticeship. He had been helping his mother hang the wash while his father watched. They talked about Renick without acknowledging he was there. It was a regular occurrence in his family. Renick remembered the awkward sinking feeling he had felt then. He felt much the same way now.

Derth seemed to be relaying much of their story to the assembly. Renick could see images from their journey through the forest and their encounter with the hunters. Most of the images were from Plyth's point of view, but a few must have come from Wrytha.

For a moment there seemed to be some discord among the dragons. Derth suggested something about hearing or understanding, and some of the other dragons did not receive it well.

"They do not understand us." Derth's words reverberated in the stillness of the dragon hall. "They deserve to know what is being said of them."

This angered many of those perched on the stone pedestals. A rumbling order silenced the growls of protest.

"Present the humans." A deep voice echoed off the walls of the cavern.

Derth turned and used one of his front claws to motion the children forward. In a low voice, he said, "Introduce yourselves."

"I'm Renick-Trusted." Renick glanced at Derth, who dipped his head in approval.

"I'm Lainey-Kind."

"And I'm Thane-Brave," Thane declared, his chest puffed out in pride.

A rumble rippled through the assembled dragons. "They are dragon-named?" one exclaimed.

"Who has dragon-named them?" The dragon at the very center of the tallest circle was watching Renick. He was a large, gold dragon with black wings.

Renick opened his mouth to reply before he remembered Derth's instructions.

Derth answered, "My great-nephew, Plyth Firetongue."

"And he claims they aided him?" the gold dragon asked.

To confirm the statement, Derth dipped his head.

"Speak," the gold dragon said, his eyes boring into Renick. "Did you indeed help the young one, Plyth Firetongue?"

"Yes," Renick answered. He rubbed his palms along his pants, wiping away the sweat.

"Why?" a different voice asked.

Renick turned to the speaker. She was a beautiful pale green with white neck spikes. He shrugged. "Plyth needed our help. He was in pain and alone."

"Lies," a red dragon hissed. "Complete and utter lies!"

At the words, Renick's stomach sank. He had no way of proving what he said was true. What would he do if they did not believe him?

"I will vouch for their honesty. They are who they profess to be. Nothing more, nothing less," Derth insisted.

Renick watched the older dragon, confused by his loyalty and fervent defense. He did not understand how they had earned such deep respect from him.

"Even so," a purple female with a shaky, unused voice said, "they could still know too much to be released. They could lead our enemies to this sanctuary."

Renick knew in his heart that he would never give away the dragons' secret if they asked for his silence. A small pang of regret hit him when he thought of never being able to share the story with his father. But his silence would be to protect the dragons, and that was more important.

"I trust them to keep our secret. All of them." Derth glanced back at Renick and the others.

Renick turned to see Thane and Lainey nod in agreement.

"There are ways to extract knowledge from unwilling informants," a stiff orange dragon offered. "That they know of our existence and how to locate us makes them dangerous, regardless of the merits of their character."

For a moment, Renick could not breathe. He remembered Horrin and how he had tried to get information. The dragons had much more power and strength at their disposal, not to mention their magic. For the first time since meeting Wrytha, Renick started to feel afraid.

"But they are so young, so innocent," a light, airy voice said.

"It makes no difference," the red dragon said. "They are still a threat. I call for their execution!"

The dragon hall erupted. Dragons flapped their wings and

sung out their agreement or shock. They ceased to talk aloud and Renick's mind filled with images and emotions. The dragons' speaking beat against Renick's head. The pain flared and exploded. He stumbled back. Lainey's small hands closed around his arm. Was she calling his name?

"Make it stop," Renick pleaded.

He felt himself being drawn away from the dragon hall. The bursts of pain lessened as the dragons voices faded from his mind. His vision cleared a little and he saw that he and Lainey were in a side passage. Thane stood with his back to them, watching Derth, who was just visible around a bend.

Lainey pressed a handful of dried leaves into his hand and commanded him to chew on them. Without complaint, Renick compiled. She then held out a waterskin to him. "Drink."

The cold water slid down his throat, carrying with it some of the numbing juice of the leaves. As the herbs took effect, Renick relaxed and leaned against the passageway wall.

"Better?" Lainey asked.

Renick smiled and nodded.

The dragons sounded their song one more time and then dispersed. Derth came to stand with them.

"So?" Lainey said in a shaky voice.

"There is disagreement among those in the Inner Circle. They have decided to choose your fate at a later time. For now, you will serve in the mines," Derth told them. Renick had the feeling that 'mines' was not the word Derth really wanted to use.

"The mines?" Thane asked. Renick could see the muscles in Thane's jaw tighten.

"It is where we send our outlaws and criminals for punishment," Derth said. Renick could feel that familiar sense of secrecy underneath the words.

"Great," Thane said.

"At least they aren't going to execute us," Renick offered.

"Not today," Thane countered.

Enslavement

Renick followed behind Derth as he led them through a series of complicated tunnels, moving ever downward. As they descended deeper into the mountains, the tunnels became more rough and constricting. Lainey became ever more wary.

"We have entered the mines," Derth told them. The mines were cold and dark. An oppressive sense of foreboding hung in the stale air. Renick felt the same shrouding he had felt when Wrytha first brought them to the city. *Secret way*, Derth's voice seemed to say in Renick's mind.

"I won't go down there," Lainey cried, shaking her head as she peered into the dim tunnel ahead.

Derth turned to look at her. A wave of pity sent a spike of pain through Renick's head. "You must," the dragon told her.

"No." Her eyes filled with tears and she started to tremble.

"Why must we?" Thane demanded. His jaw set and his stance firm.

"Thane-Brave, the best way for you to gain freedom is to cooperate," Derth said.

"So we're just supposed to roll over and play dead?" Thane crossed his arms. Renick half expected him to stomp his foot in protest as well.

Lainey let out a small cry. "It isn't fair!"

"It'll be okay." Renick held out his hand and patted Lainey's arm. "We have to trust Derth and Wrytha—it's our only hope."

Lainey tore her arm away from him and buried her face in her hands.

Thane touched her shoulder and when she looked up, he offered Lainey his arm. "We'll be with you every step."

With a final squeeze of her eyes, Lainey nodded. She clutched at Thane's arm the whole way. The long tunnel leading into the mines eventually opened up into a wide chamber with a low ceiling. Glowing orbs offered scant illumination that cast everything in an odd orange glow. They were delivered to a hulking gray dragon named Boren. He seemed to grumble under his breath when Derth explained the situation.

"Out loud, please," Derth reminded the other dragon with a meaningful tilt of his head.

"So the Inner Circle leaves me to clean up their mess for them again, huh?" the large dragon said with a huff. "It is enough to have a murderer and a thief on my hands, let alone three humans."

Before he left, Derth turned to Lainey. "I will be pressing for them to decide your fate as soon as possible. I still hope to persuade them to show mercy. Lainey-Kind, it will only be for a short while."

Lainey smiled weakly at him. Her free hand stopped trembling, but she still held onto Thane's arm. With a slight bob of his head, Derth turned and left them in the mines.

"Very well," Boren said. "Come with me. Let us see if I can find somewhere to put you to good use." He lumbered down a side passage that was even dimmer than the chamber they left behind.

"We have to go down there?" Lainey whimpered.

Thane extracted his arm from her grip and wrapped it around her shoulders. "Come on, Lainey," he said, "you can do this."

She looked up at Thane and smiled. Renick reached out and touched her arm. "We'll do it together," he promised. Lainey's smile brightened. The three of them followed after Boren.

The large dragon led them down a tunnel wide enough for four dragons to walk abreast. With rough-hewn walls and jagged floors, the tunnel seemed newer than the ones above them. For a time, the hollowed-out area angled downward, but after only a short while, it leveled out and started to narrow. When the passageway dead-ended in a pile of rubble, it was just large enough for two dragons of Boren's size.

In the center of the pile of rocks and dust, two dragons labored to dig through a rock wall. They breathed fire on the wall until it glowed red and hot, then raked their claws over the heated portion, causing chunks of rock to fall away. In a pair of alcoves across from each other, two more dragons stood watch over the prisoners as they worked.

"Dig here," Boren said and left.

"Here we are, our punishment for—what was it?" Thane looked over at Renick. "That's right, saving the little squirming worm."

"Thane," Lainey admonished, her voice soft and weak.

"Lainey's right. My mother always says you can't change the winds—just roll up your sleeves and get the work done."

Renick eyed the guard dragons. They looked stern and alert. The dragon prisoners had paused in their digging and were watching them.

"All right, then," Renick said and rubbed his hands together. "What're we mining for?"

A sound very much like a chuckle emanated from the smaller of the two prisoners. It was hard for Renick to tell what color he was under the layer of dirt covering his scales. The dim lighting did not help much, either.

"Not mining." The prisoner chuckled again. "Just digging." The dragon turned back to his work. His laugh grew in pitch until it was almost a wail as he tore viciously into the rock wall.

The other prisoner dragon just watched them with dull eyes.

"Do not mind Hyngarth," one of the guards said. "He is not right in the head."

"What's the point of digging if you aren't mining?" Thane asked.

The guard tilted his crimson head, but did not answer.

"Secret way," Hyngarth hissed. "Under mountain, under trees, secret way out." He let loose a stream of flame that danced wildly around the rock wall.

"Prisoners dig for punishment." The other guard, who was a striking green on white, said.

"Ah," Thane said, not sounding the least bit satisfied.

"I'm Renick-Trusted," Renick offered to the two guard dragons.

"Guards do not speak to prisoners unless absolutely necessary," the green guard intoned.

Thane looked over at Renick, who shrugged.

"I guess we get to work, then." Renick examined the pile of rubble. Most of the broken rocks were too massive for them to move, even if they worked together. But there were plenty of smaller rocks and dirt that they could shift. He bent down and picked up a cooled rock about the size of his head. He turned to the crimson guard. "Where do I put this?"

The dragon moved aside, revealing another passageway. Renick trudged down the tunnel, which proved to be quite short. It ended abruptly at a fissure in the ground. There was a small area that had been hollowed out above the crack. Renick wondered if it ran further out on either side, but he could not tell in the almost complete darkness.

Renick lobbed his rock into the crevasse. On his way back, he found Thane and Lainey standing at the opening to the tunnel. Thane was balancing a large boulder between his knee and the wall. Lainey was clutching a small rock and staring into the darkness.

"She won't go in," Thane said.

Renick nodded. Thane picked up his load and headed down the tunnel.

Gently, Renick pried Lainey's fingers away from the rock, which was not much bigger than her two fists. He set it down next to the opening. "How about this. You carry the rocks here, and Thane and I will take them into the tunnel, okay?"

Her eyes flickered to his face. "You won't leave me?"

"One of us will stay with you. We'll take turns." Renick put a hand on her shoulder.

Lainey nodded and scurried over to the rubble. Together they rolled a large boulder to the tunnel opening. Just as they settled it against the wall, Thane emerged from the darkness.

"I've got this," he said and turned to head down again. "I'm working on a plan," he added in a whisper.

"Let me know how it goes," Renick said, not at all optimistic.

Returning to the colossal pile of rubble, Lainey started filling Renick's arms with smaller rocks. She balanced them neatly in a small mound that reached up to his chin. Renick had to walk carefully along the uneven ground to avoid spilling her work. When Thane appeared once again, Renick took his cargo down to the crevasse. On the way back, he had to flatten himself against the tunnel wall when Hyngarth came barreling down the tunnel pushing a boulder as tall as Renick. The crazy dragon howled as the rock fell into the darkness, and then he rushed back up the tunnel. Renick followed slowly behind.

The cold air of the cave soon became a comfort as beads of sweat formed on Renick's forehead and neck.

The hours wore on. Thane would take a few trips and then rest with Lainey while Renick took a turn heading down to the chasm. Back and forth. Lift and drop. Stone and rock and dirt and grime. And still the hours wore on. Renick's hands were soon raw and covered in small scrapes. His nose filled with dirt until it was the only thing he could smell. His eyes ached from the lack of light. More hours passed.

Finally, when every inch of Renick's body screamed for a respite from the monotonous strain, Boren reappeared. "I am told you need to be fed," he grumbled. "Come with me."

The sound of rocks tumbling to the ground made Renick start and almost lose his hold on his awkward load. He turned to see Thane brushing dust from his arms as he hurried after Boren. Lainey pushed past Renick, knocking his elbow. With a sigh, Renick relinquished his hold on the rock and followed after the others.

Boren led them back to the chamber where they had met. In one corner sat their packs. Renick and his friends settled themselves on the ground in a small circle. Lainey passed out their waterskins while Thane dug in a rucksack for some dried meat.

"Sure wish they'd give us some other food." Thane handed out their meager fare.

"Wonder if they'll let us take a bath," Lainey said between bites.

Renick was going to reply, but his words were drowned out by a loud rumbling noise.

Proven

The ground and walls and ceiling shook.

"Stay here," Boren ordered as he stumbled back down the passageway.

"Wait—" The sound of boulders falling swallowed the rest of Renick's words. A cloud of dust billowed from the passageway, engulfing them. For two terrifying heartbeats, the world was nothing but brown dust and darkness.

All was still and quiet.

Renick shook the dirt from his hair and passed his sleeve over his face. "What was that?"

"Cave-in," Thane croaked, and then started coughing.

Lainey looked up. There were streaks on her face where the dirt stuck to her tears. She held her canteen out to Thane. He took a large gulp of water and the coughing subsided.

Hyngarth burst through the tunnel opening. "Free, free, free, free," he panted. He turned toward Renick and the others, dancing around a little. "Come, we free. Come, come, come, come, come, come." With a fit of laughter, he tore down the tunnel that led out of the mines.

Following more slowly, the other prisoner that had been digging with them emerged. He paused and glanced at Renick. A chill danced down Renick's back.

I will avenge her, an eerie voiced whispered in Renick's mind.

The dragon moved on.

Renick shook his head to clear the oppressive gloom that hung over him. "Where're the guards?" He turned to Thane and Lainey, who were just staring at him. "And Boren?"

He watched the opening of the passageway intently. Nothing stirred as the moments inched by.

Renick jumped to his feet. "Come on." He did not wait for the others to follow and plunged into the tunnel.

Halfway down, his progress was halted by a wall of rubble sloping gently up to the ceiling. A low moan and the sound of shifting rock drew Renick's attention. Boren lay on one side of the passageway with a small layer of sand and rock dusted over him. When Renick tried to speak with him, the dragon did not respond.

Lainey fell to her knees next to where Renick crouched. She placed her ear against Boren's massive jaws. "He's breathing," she reported.

"Are the guards still back there?" Thane asked, studying the wall of debris.

"I didn't see them come out," Lainey answered.

"Do you think they survived?" Renick tried to swallow the lump growing in his throat.

Thane moved to the blockage and examined it. "There's a gap here," he said, pointing to a place near the tunnel wall. "But I can't see anything."

Renick joined Thane and peered into the blackness. "If they're completely buried ..."

A warm hand rested on his shoulder. "There could be a cavity, an air pocket, on the other side of that gap," Thane said. "There may still be hope."

"But how do we tell?" Lainey's hands busily worked at brushing the dust and rubble from Boren's immobile body.

"We need to make a torch." Thane turned and ran up the tunnel. He came back a few moments later with their packs. Fishing in his, he pulled out some flint and steel.

Lainey stood and placed her fists on her hips. "And just

what do you expect us to do with that?"

"Light the torch." Thane looked up at the ceiling in exasperation.

"What torch?" She tilted her head at him.

Thane looked around the tunnel. Renick followed his gaze. Rocks, rubble, dust, dragon lantern, stone, and more rocks. Nothing to fuel a torch with.

"The dragon lanterns!" Renick ran to the cavern wall and wrapped his hands around one of the glowing orbs as best he could. Using all the strength his tired arms had, he pulled. The dragon lantern did not budge. Thane's large hands joined Renick's and together they tried again to dislodge the orb.

"They are held there by magic," Boren said, his voice weak and rasping.

Renick turned. "We need to see if anyone's on the other side of the cave-in. Can you release the lantern?"

A rumble, halfway between a growl and a hum, rippled through Boren's throat. A nearby orb fell from its place and rolled to Renick's feet. The orb was about the size of his head, but weighed practically nothing when he lifted it.

Back at the small opening in the wall of rubble, Renick pushed the dragon lantern through the gap. He shoved it as far as he could without crawling into the hole. The orb started to roll downhill. Soon it dipped out of sight and Renick heard a dull clank. The orb's light illuminated a small opening and reflected off a set of scales.

"I see one of them," Renick called. Boren's head appeared at Renick's elbow. Jumping, Renick backed away. The dragon peered into the chamber beyond the cave-in and then studied the rubble that blocked their way.

"The cave-in is too unstable. We will not be able to shift the rock. I am afraid if they are alive in there, soon they will not be." Boren hung his head and moved away.

"You can't dig them out?" Renick asked.

"We cannot. We do not have your delicate hands, digging for dragons is a bit more brute force."

"What about your magic?" Renick asked. "Can't you use

that to move the rubble?"

Boren shook his head. "Our magic changes and heals—it does not move or destroy. I am afraid there is nothing to be done."

"No!" Lainey said.

"We're going to save them." Thane turned to look at Renick. "What should we do?"

Renick felt as if the entire pile of fallen rock had settled on his back and shoulders. He shifted his weight from one foot to the other and then back again. Renick wanted to shrug, but resisted the urge—this was no time for uncertainty. He looked back through the gap. "We dig them out," he said.

"That is a dangerous endeavor." Boren was watching him very closely.

"I know." Renick paused to look at Thane and Lainey for support. "Right, then. Someone should probably coordinate from the other side." He rubbed his hands on the sides of his pants and moved to the opening. He only made it a few feet into the tunnel before his shoulders hit against a rock. Angling his body, Renick attempted to move forward again, only to receive another bruise. The third attempt resulted in a shower of dirt and rocks. He threw his arms up in front of his face as a shield, but still got a good portion of the dirt in his eyes, mouth, and nose.

Renick dropped his head and started moving backwards. "I don't fit," he said in response to Thane's questioning look.

"Well, if you don't, I definitely can't." Thane looked into the gap. "And I don't think we can widen it without it collapsing."

"I think you're right." Renick dusted some of the dirt out of his hair.

"I'll do it," Lainey said from behind them. Her voice shook a little.

Renick turned. Lainey's breathing was slow and even. Her arms hung down by her sides and her hands were clenched in fists.

"I'll do it," she repeated with more confidence.

"Lainey," Renick started to protest.

She looked at him with resolve burning in her eyes. "You'll come for me."

Renick nodded. "We'll always come for you."

Lainey took a deep breath and walked up to the hole. With both hands, she lifted the strap of her healer's pouch over her head and held it out. Renick took it. She stood for a moment, facing the darkness.

"Just keep going," Thane said. "It'll be more difficult if you try to come back."

Without turning to look at Thane, Lainey nodded. Then she climbed into the gap and started crawling to the chamber beyond.

"Plyth should have named *her* Brave," Thane commented as he watched Lainey's progress.

Renick shook his head. "No, he named her right. It's her kindness that helps her forget her fear."

They watched in silence. Lainey moved slowly at first, inching her way along. She would flinch and whimper any time a portion of the tunnel would shift. Renick could hear the faint whisper of her mumbling to herself.

"You can make it, Lainey," he called to her.

This seemed to inspire her—the mumbling stopped and she started to move at a faster pace.

"Almost there," Thane said just as Lainey disappeared from their view.

"I'm through," her quiet voice called at last. Renick could see her face through the opening. She waved at him and then ducked away. He could hear her moving around in the adjoining chamber. Lainey's face came back into the circle of dim light. "Both the guards are here. One's injured, but awake and mostly okay. The other's partially buried. He won't respond to me."

"What do you need?" Thane asked.

"Lots of water. And bandages. And I need my healer's pouch. More light wouldn't hurt, either."

Renick nodded and tossed her healer's pouch down to her

while Thane collected a second orb, which Boren dislodged for him. Renick turned to Boren. "We need water, and lots of it. And anything Lainey can use to bandage the dragons' wounds."

The dragon dipped his head. "Anything else?" he asked.

With a shrug, Renick looked over his shoulder at Thane.

"I don't suppose you have any tools for digging?" Thane asked.

Boren laughed. "Not that a human could use."

"Could your magic make them from the rock?"

The dragon tilted his head. "It might. What shape do you need?"

Renick and Thane set about drawing shapes in the dirt of the shovels and wheelbarrow they would need. Boren touched large chunks of stone with his nose and hummed. The stone shifted like sand and took on a new form. The dragon made the shovels first. Thane collected these and set them aside. Next Boren worked on the wheelbarrow, forming the bucket and handle and then the wheels and an axle. Together Thane and Renick assembled the pieces.

"Excellent," Renick proclaimed when they were done. Boren and Thane nodded in agreement.

"We'll still have to do some of it by hand," Thane warned when they were finished.

"All right, then." Renick rolled up his sleeves. "We should get to work."

Renick did not know how long they toiled. Time was swallowed up with the endless shifting of rock. Slow and steady like the water trickling down the walls, they made progress through the pile of rubble. More than once, Lainey's warning cries were all that saved them from another cave-in. Renick's eyes and mouth filled with dirt. He did not notice the cold or the sweat. His raw hands gripped the rough handles of his shovel and the sharp edges of the bits of stone. Vaguely he remembered receiving food and water from somewhere. At one point, he noticed that his hands had been wrapped with little strips of cloth and he wondered who had done it.

They did not rest.

On and on they dug. Boren formed an aquifer to direct water from somewhere above. The liquid was cold and refreshing when Renick lifted a handful to his mouth. He cleared his throat of dirt and poured some of the water over his head. The clean, renewed feeling did not last long. The oppressive repetition of the digging soon returned the layer of sweat and grime to his face.

Once they had made it through to the chamber where Lainey tended the two fallen guards, they set to work freeing the one that was trapped. Behind him, Renick heard bodies moving as Boren and Lainey assisted in removing the first guard from the collapsed passageway. Still, Renick and Thane moved rock and stone, stone and rock. This task proved more difficult. They could not let any of the rocks shift over the dragon for fear of causing further injury. Lainey helped direct their movements, her voice and hands always steady.

Renick felt something press against his back. He turned to see Boren. "Be done, young ones. This one will not likely survive, despite your efforts."

"No matter what the odds," Renick told him, "we'll try."

Boren withdrew, and Renick did not know how much more time passed. Renick's hands, sore and bleeding from all the work, scooped up a pile of rocks. He moved them aside and when he went to collect more, he saw the end of the dragon's tail. He looked up, surprised. Meeting Thane's gaze, he said, "done."

Boren led two dragons to retrieve the uncovered guard. They gently dragged him out of the mines.

Their task complete, Renick sank to the ground. Lainey's face, blurry and smudged, appeared in his view. She pressed something to his lips.

"Drink," she commanded, and he obeyed.

"So tired." Renick's head rolled forward as he succumbed to exhaustion.

Air

Renick woke when cool, fresh air brushed against his cheek. He opened his eyes and found himself lying on his back outside under a sky filled with stars. He sat up. Around him was a conglomeration of sticks, goose down, and other soft materials. Another dragon's nest. This one was much larger than Wrytha's and stood out in the open near the top of one of the mountain peaks.

"You will spend the night here," Boren said. Renick looked up to see the large dragon standing just outside the nest. A sleeping Lainey was lying across Boren's neck. Standing, Renick moved to help Thane slide her off. In the process, she stirred and woke up.

Lainey looked around. She took a long, deep breath and a small sob of joy escaped her. "Air."

"Lainey-Kind, after your deeds tonight, I will not let them confine you like that again," Boren promised.

The light from the moon made the tears that filled Lainey's eyes sparkle. "Thank you."

"You all are welcome in my home for as long as you are with us." Boren dipped his head and then moved a little ways off.

Thane extended his arm. From his hand hung Renick's

pack. When Renick took it from him, Thane found a spot a safe distance from the nest and started a small fire. With their beds laid out, Lainey fished in their rucksacks for some food.

"Anyone hungry?" she asked.

Renick shook his head.

"I'm too tired to eat." Thane stretched his arms and yawned.

"Just as well—we're running out of food." Lainey closed her pack.

"I will see to that," Boren said. He was spread out near a cave opening that probably led to the dragon city, as if protecting them from its occupants.

Lainey tried vainly to brush the dirt and tangles from her hair with her fingers. "Ugh," she exclaimed, "I need a bath!"

"There is a stream just around that bend. It will be cold, but will do the job," Boren told her.

Lainey jumped up and headed in the direction the dragon had indicated. Just before she disappeared behind the bend, she looked back over her shoulder. "Don't let them come peek," she told Boren, who chuckled in response.

A little while later, Lainey returned. Her hair was wet and she was humming.

Thane stood and bowed to her. "Now that milady has finished, she won't mind if we loathsome men tarnish her bath, will she?"

Lainey just rolled her eyes at him and settled on the ground next to Renick. Thane was back in almost no time at all. His hair was wet too and he had his shirt slung over his shoulder, his sword, belt, and scabbard clutched in one hand. Lainey eyed him as he sat down.

"Milord should dress himself properly before entering the presence of a lady." She smirked at him.

The corner of Thane's mouth twitched as he pulled his shirt over his head.

"Keep an eye on these two, will you?" Renick asked Boren. "They could eat each other alive at any second."

Boren tossed his head and released a small puff of smoke in

amusement as Renick turned away.

It did not take long for Renick to reach the mountain stream. He dipped his fingers in the running water. It was ice cold. Taking off his shirt, he did his best to wash out his hair. He splashed the water on his chest and arms. The cool water relieved the burning ache in his muscles. It did not seem like a good idea to get his shirt wet, since he lacked a spare. So he just did his best to shake the dirt out and pulled it back over his head. Feeling refreshed, but still dirty, he headed back.

When Renick returned to their little camp, a red dragon sat waiting. Renick thought he recognized the dragon as the one that called for their execution in the dragon court. His steps slowed and he cast his eyes around to find Lainey and Thane sitting by the fire. Renick sat with them.

Renick looked to Thane, his eyebrows scrunched together in a question. Thane frowned and shook his head slightly. One corner of Lainey's mouth twitched and she scrunched up her nose. Apparently Renick had not missed much.

"Renick-Trusted, Thane-Brave, and Lainey-Kind," the red dragon said, "I am Grane Redthorne of the Second Circle, and tonight you saved my son, Flyn Thorntail."

The three of them exchanged looks. "We're glad we could help," Renick offered.

"For three of your kind to show such valor when you could have fled with the other prisoners and obtained your freedom—it astonishes me." Grane shook his head.

"We had to help," Lainey said.

"That is just it, Lainey-Kind. You did not have to help. Nothing but that which is inside you compelled you to assist my son and the other dragon trapped in the cave-in. You showed qualities that I believed to be gone from your race entirely." A rumble started deep in the dragon's throat. "In fact, I have seen them fade from my kind as well." He looked at each of them. "I am forever in your debt." He turned to leave. "I will speak for you."

Grane left, descending back into the mountain through the cave entrance where Boren sat.

"That was ... interesting," Thane said.

"Apparently he appreciated what we did," Lainey commented.

Renick shrugged. "To be honest, it never occurred to me that we could've just left."

"Even if it had," Lainey said, shaking her head, "you could never have left those dragons down there."

"You two helped," Renick said. His cheeks started to feel hot.

"What you three have done," Boren said, "has shown many of us that you are not like any other humans we have ever known."

"You must not know very good people," Lainey said.

Boren made a noise between a hum and a chuckle. "We mostly know the hunters."

Lainey grimaced. "I wouldn't like humans either if they were the only ones I knew."

They all laughed at this.

"Rest, children. I have a feeling tomorrow will be a big day for you."

Renick leaned back and watched the stars hanging in the black sky above. Every inch of his body was weary, but his mind kept churning thoughts, and he could not quiet them. He focused on Lainey's shallow breathing and Thane's slight snore hoping the sounds would distract him. Despite all his efforts, sleep still eluded him.

The soft sound of dirt moving under something made Renick sit up. He turned to see Derth had arrived and was sitting watching him.

"You are still awake. What troubles you?" Derth asked.

"I'm ..." Renick tried to find the words to describe how he was feeling. When his search turned up nothing, he thought of his jumbled emotions. He felt homesick and lonely without his large family. At the same time, he was enjoying the relative solitude of being away from them. He worried about tomorrow—about the fate the new day would bring. He felt excited about the new friendships he was forming with Thane,

Lainey, and Plyth. But mostly, he was curious about the dragons.

He wrapped all this up into one thought, one image, and tried to show it to Derth.

The old dragon cocked his head and made a sound that reminded him of his father when Renick or his siblings surprised him. "I think I understand," Derth said. "A lot has happened to you today."

Renick crossed his legs underneath him and shrugged. "It's all so different."

"You mean, intelligent dragons?"

"Yes," Renick said, nodding.

"And here I thought you were adjusting well." Derth chuckled. "You did, after all, rescue two of our kind."

Renick shook his head. "I ..." He stopped. He thought what he had been about to say was prideful and might not entirely be true.

"My boy, it is not pride when you are honest with yourself." Derth moved closer and bent his neck down and around so his head was level with Renick's. Derth's deep eyes met his. "Even though I have known you a short time, I know what you feel is true. You would have done the same for any man or beast. So would Lainey-Kind and Thane-Brave. That is why Plyth trusts you—because you are worthy of such trust."

Renick felt uncomfortable. He squirmed and tried to find a better way to sit. Derth held his gaze, never turning away. "I don't even know how I earned it," Renick said.

Derth sat back, another laugh rumbling in his long throat. "That, my boy, is precisely the point. Do not worry so about tomorrow. I believe your worth will be acknowledged by the Inner Circle."

Renick smiled. He was a little relieved. His other thoughts and worries started to melt away and left him with just one. "What happened?" he asked.

"What do you mean?"

"What happened between the humans and the dragons?"

Derth sighed, and a trail of smoke floated up from

between his teeth. "Much of that story is dangerous to tell." A growl thundered in the dragon's chest. "We fell prey to the greed of mankind. They desired our magic at a greater speed and capacity than we would provide. So they sought to enslave us. But the ancestors of the mute dragons saw to it that their endeavor failed."

"You mean, the mute dragons are like you? They can talk?" Renick said.

"No." Derth tilted his head. "As I told you before, they do not have the capacity to speak. It has been absent from their bloodlines for generations."

"And they don't have magic?"

Derth shook his head. "No, Renick-Trusted, they do not have magic."

"That's why the hunters seek your kind. Because you do." Renick thought back to the terrible hunger in Horrin's eyes.

"Yes."

"We're not all like that," Renick said. He placed his head in his hands. "It's such a shame."

"A shame?"

"We could learn so much from you. Do so much together. I regret that my ancestors took that away from me—from us." Renick swept his arm out to take in Thane and Lainey and anyone else in the world.

"Regret." Derth bobbed his head a few times. "That is a good name for it." The old dragon looked up at the stars. "Until I met you three, I did not feel this way. My whole life I have hated, even feared, your kind." Derth looked back to Renick. "But you have changed me."

Renick did not know how to respond. He felt an odd tingling sensation in his stomach. Eventually he settled on shrugging again.

"You three have opened my eyes. Your kind think of our mute brothers and sisters as cattle, but we have thought even less of you. You aided Plyth. You saved the two dragons in the mines. All at great cost to yourselves." Derth paused. He seemed unsure if he wanted to continue. Renick waited patiently. "These are things I am not sure many dragons would do. Renick-Trusted, you regret what your kind is lacking because of their greed. I regret what my kind turns its back on because of pride."

"Do you think the wounds can be mended?" Renick asked, hope flickering in his heart.

Derth did not answer right away. At length, he spoke, "If you had asked me that question yesterday, I would have said no. Then I believed the wounds to be too old, too deep. But today, I think there is a chance that with time, they can be healed. Or at least forgotten."

Renick smiled. "I'd like to think you're right." Silently he promised himself to do all he could to repair the damage done so long ago, though he did not know how he would even start.

"Now, Renick-Trusted, you must rest. Tomorrow will be yet another big day for you. It will be important to have all your wits about you." Derth stood to leave.

"Derth," Renick called. The dragon stopped and turned to look back at him. "Tell Plyth good night for me."

The older dragon just stared at Renick for a long time. Then he dipped his head and disappeared underground.

Renick lay back and with one final look at the night sky, fell asleep.

The Gift

Renick bent over Lainey's sleeping form and gently shook her shoulder. "Lainey, wake up." With a moan, she rolled over and opened her gray eyes.

"What?" Her voice was heavy with sleep.

"They want us in the infrem ... infirmry ... in ... The dragon healer is summoning us," Renick explained.

"What? Why?" Lainey moved to sit up and he assisted her. "We aren't hurt."

"Hurry, young ones," Derth said from his position near the entrance to the dragon city. "There isn't much time." His dark scales blended so well with the rock in the darkness of night that Renick could only see the moonlight reflecting in the dragon's eyes.

Lainey, still not fully awake, leaned on Renick's arm. Slowly they moved forward, following Derth and Thane down into the dragon city.

Derth led them through the twisting tunnels to a large chamber well lit by dozens of dragon lanterns clinging to the ceiling. Dragons of all ages and sizes lay in neat rows throughout the open area. Between them, other dragons moved back and forth, sometimes stopping to talk with the ill, sometimes touching them with their snouts.

"This is the infirmary," Derth told them.

A dragon with orange scales and white spikes approached them. She was small compared to the others of the Dragon Kind. Dipping her head low, she introduced herself as Mryx Clawmender. "I have been caring for the two dragons you saved yesterday."

"How are they?" Lainey asked eagerly. She rubbed the remaining sleep from her eyes as she scanned the room looking for them. Renick did not think he would recognize them in the sea of dragons.

"Flyn Thorntail is recovering slowly, but surely. He will only be in our care for a few days," Mryx answered, bending her head low so it was level with Lainey's.

"And the other?" Renick asked. A knot had formed in his stomach and threatened to swallow the last of his words.

Mryx's eyes saddened. "Junther Swiftwing won't survive the night."

The knot in Renick's stomach turned hard and cold. He found it difficult to breathe.

"Oh, no," Lainey gasped and covered her mouth, tears filling her eyes.

"Have we been brought here to be punished?" Thane said, his voice quiet and laced with an emotion Renick could not identify. Turning, Renick saw that though Thane's left hand rested on Lainey's shoulder to give her comfort, the other was tensely wrapped around the hilt of his sword.

"No." Mryx shook her head at them. "Quite the contrary. Junther wishes to speak to the three of you."

She turned and started making her way between the rows of sick and injured dragons. Renick and the others followed, though Derth remained behind. As they neared the other side of the cavern, Renick noticed a row of dark openings along it. It was to one of these openings that Mryx directed them. Behind the opening was an alcove filled with half a dozen dragons. Most of them stood clustered around Junther, the fallen guard who lay in the center of the small room.

Mryx entered the alcove first. Bending down, she told

Junther, "I have brought them to you."

The guard lifted his head and turned to look at Renick and the others. Renick recognized him as the kind guard that had spoken briefly with them.

"Let me see you." It sounded as if Junther had to force out each word.

Lainey stepped forward, unaffected by the atmosphere of sorrow and inevitability. She knelt near the dragon's head where it lay on a small mound of goose down.

Renick shuffled around so Junther could see him.

"You too, Thane-Brave." Mryx gave Thane a gentle nudge with her nose.

Thane bumped into Renick's shoulder as he sidled up next to him. "Sorry," he whispered. Thane's face was pale and drawn, and he kept adjusting his clothes and fidgeting with his sword.

"I want to thank the three of you," Junther said.

"For what?" Renick asked. "We didn't save you. You're still going to die."

Junther shifted his position before responding. "Yes, but I would have died alone. Because of you three, I was given a chance to say my good-byes and to die surrounded by my family."

Renick could understand that. A memory from the day of the flyer crash came to his mind. He remembered falling, seeing the trees and sky spiraling around him, and wishing his last words to his family had been different.

"I want to do something to repay you, but I have little to offer." Junther looked at each of them in turn.

Lainey shook her head. "You owe us nothing for our failure."

"Dear Lainey-Kind, you did not fail. Sometimes our success is not measured by the outcome, but by our efforts. You especially gave a great effort to save me. You conquered the dark in an attempt to save me from it." Junther leaned forward and breathed on Lainey's forehead. "And that is success enough to me."

Lainey's hand went to her face as she wiped at her eyes.

"I have little time left. I will let the others speak to you of their matters." Junther stopped to groan in pain. Mryx placed her snout on his neck, and he sighed with relief.

"Lainey-Kind, I gift you my heart stone when I am gone. Use this gift to heal and aid others." A rumble started in Junther's chest and rippled out through his throat. A wave of white smoke washed over Lainey, tossing her hair and settling on her shoulders before dissipating.

"What just happened?" Thane asked in a sharp voice.

"Hush. It is done," Mryx said. "Now, young ones, you must wait outside. Junther wishes to spend his final moments with those he loves."

"I'm fine, Thane," Lainey reassured him, motioning for them to follow Mryx's instructions.

Renick turned to leave following, behind Thane. When they exited the alcove, Thane stopped and turned to face the opening. Renick leaned against the wall next to him. It took a few moments for Lainey to follow. Her head was down, but Renick could see the tears between the gaps in her hanging bangs.

"You all right?" he asked.

Ever so slightly, Lainey nodded her head. "What's…what's a heart stone?"

Renick shrugged. "I don't know."

"Don't you know a story about one?"

"Yeah, there has to be some little tidbit about it in that big head of yours." The corners of Thane's mouth twitched as he spoke.

"Nope, I can't think of any reference to a heart stone. Or any kind of stone, really." Renick paused a moment. He could sense that this was something important. It tugged at his memory. "But …"

"But what?" Thane grabbed Renick's shoulders. "I don't plan on just standing by and letting who-knows-what happen to my friend."

Mryx's head appeared from the opening to Junther's alcove.

"Lainey-Kind, you are needed inside."

Lainey looked up at Renick and then Thane. Her eyes spoke of uncertainty.

Mryx moved closer. "Come, child."

Thane stepped between Lainey and the dragon, drawing his sword as he did so. "Leave her alone."

"Wait." Renick stepped forward. "I ... I think it's okay, Thane. It won't hurt her."

Thane considered him for a moment, then lowered his sword. "I trust you, Renick."

Lainey nodded. "I trust you too." Without any further hesitation, she disappeared after Mryx.

"Out with it, Renick," Thane said.

"The legends talk of dragons giving the final, or greatest, gift. This gift grants long life and such to the receiver. Remember the story of Louren? According to that, and several other stories, a dragon's heart is magical or has magical properties," Renick replied.

"So?"

"So, unless I'm wrong, a dragon's heart stone is that final gift and will grant Lainey long life and maybe even more." Renick could feel excitement tingling in his fingers. All the pieces were starting to fall together. The world around him started to make more sense.

"Then let's hope you aren't wrong," Thane mumbled.

Movement on the other side of the chamber caught Renick's attention, and he saw Derth coming toward them.

"What happened?" the old dragon asked. His voice was laden with foreboding.

"Junther's dying," Renick said. He could hear the nervousness in his own voice.

"Yes, yes, I know. But Mryx sent for me, so it must have been something else. Where is Lainey?" Derth tossed his head back and forth—whether in agitation or to search for the absent girl, Renick could not tell.

Lainey emerged from the alcove, cupping a glowing stone about half the size of her palm in her hands. The yellow light reflected off her awe filled eyes.

"What has he done?" Derth whispered under his breath.

"Is that ..." Renick started, but could not finish.

"Junther's heart stone," Lainey whispered. "Mryx cut open his chest and had ... me ... get it."

That was when Renick noticed the blood coating her hands.

"He gifted it to you?" Derth asked.

Lainey nodded.

"Hold it to your chest, Lainey-Kind." Derth's tone was short and tense.

"What? Why?" She looked up at the dragon.

"Just do as you are told. Hurry, you would not want to waste such a precious gift." Derth was watching her closely. A torrent of complicated emotions churned like waves around him. Renick staggered a little when they struck his mind.

Lainey did as she was told and clutched the stone to her heart.

"It has to touch your skin," Derth snapped at her.

She looked up, her cheeks coloring. Derth's posture relaxed. "I am sorry, Lainey-Kind. Here." He moved to stand beside her to provide a shield, and then turned his head away.

Renick heard Mryx's voice from behind Derth. "Ah, good. You got the bonding process started. Thank you, Derth."

"You could not have mentioned this in your message?" Derth growled.

"I am sorry, but I was a little preoccupied," Mryx said in return. "Yes, there, Lainey. Now hold it to your skin and I will graft it in place."

Yellow light flashed from behind Derth. Renick turned his head to shade his eyes. With a few pulses, the light faded away. Derth withdrew, revealing Lainey standing with empty hands, watching Renick and Thane. A dull point of yellow light shone from beneath her blouse, just below her collarbone.

"It feels ... warm," Lainey said, a soft smile touching the edges of her mouth.

Renick remembered a line from an old poem and whispered it aloud to the group: "'Shining forth like sunshine dawning, gift of dragon, gift of light.'"

Lainey's smile widened. "That's exactly it."

"What just happened?" Thane asked. Renick was not sure if the sharp undertone to Thane's words was fear or concern, but it was probably a little of both.

"In short, Junther gifted his heart stone, which grants magical power, to Lainey-Kind," Derth said.

"Magic?" Renick, Thane, and Lainey all said at once.

"There is not time to discuss this now. We must return you to Boren's nest." He turned and added under his breath, "I wish someone had warned me what Junther was up to." Derth stopped and look back at them. "Come now. It is not safe for you three here."

Turmoil

"Tell us what's going on," Thane demanded once they were back at Boren's nest.

"Just a moment," Boren, who had been waiting there for them, said. "We need a few others present before we continue. Derth and I do not know everything."

Derth turned to look at Boren, a small bit of flame simmering between his teeth. "We don't?"

Lainey swayed slightly and Renick moved to support her. A small shock of energy ran through his arms when he touched her.

"I'm all right." She tried to wave him off. Renick, still holding her arm though his fingers buzzed, led her to a rock Thane had rolled over for her. Lainey sat gratefully and pressed her hand to the stone hidden under her shirt.

"Is she going to be okay?" Thane asked, looking up at Derth.

"Yes," Derth said in a soft voice. "She is fine. Right now, her body is trying to absorb the magic from Junther's stone. She will be weak for a few days—nothing more."

"The others are here," Boren said.

A squeal echoed from the cave entrance, and right behind it followed Plyth, bounding toward them. He ran circles around

Renick's feet, almost knocking him over. Plyth leapt into the air and hovered inches from Thane's face. With a happy bark, he licked the stunned boy and then settled onto Lainey's lap.

Lainey laughed. "Hello to you, too."

Derth glared over at Wrytha, who was now sitting next to Boren. "We have important matters to discuss."

"He insisted, Derth. Besides, those matters concern him as well." Wrytha tossed her head.

"Sit, young ones," Grane's voice said from the darkness just beyond the opening that led to the dragon city. He appeared moments later, his red scales like fire in the early morning sunlight. "We have many important matters to discuss."

Derth immediately launched a volley of what Renick could only guess were dragon insults at Grane. The other dragons responded to Derth's anger in kind. The sudden influx of dragon speech sent lances of pain through Renick's head as he tried to keep up with it all.

"Not so loud, please!" he called when the pain became unbearable.

The dragons all fell silent. Wrytha stepped forward and placed her nose on Renick's head. A warmth spread from the point of contact down to his shoulders, erasing the pain.

"Thank you." Renick gasped. He noticed that he was leaning against someone and turned to see Thane supporting him. Renick gave the older boy a thank-you nod, and Thane returned the gesture.

"We will speak aloud and I will mediate." Boren looked pointedly at Derth. "We do not want to overwhelm them. They have been through enough and need answers more than confusion."

"A good plan," Wrytha agreed.

"Hmm .... where to begin," Boren said as Renick and Thane settled themselves on the ground near where Lainey sat.

"How about with the stone?" Lainey offered.

Boren dipped his head. "Very good, Lainey. Derth, you are the one with the most knowledge of these things."

"Very well." Derth shifted a little before continuing. Renick could feel him gathering and sorting his thoughts. "Each dragon has a bony mass just above their heart. We call it the heart stone because of its shape and location. This stone contains all of our magic. In the early ages, the victor of a fight would steal the loser's stone and add it to his own, increasing his strength and power."

"What happens when a dragon loses his stone?" Renick wondered aloud.

"They die," Derth said with a growl. "This custom ended during the time of enlightenment. It is considered a grievous crime to kill a dragon for his heart stone. However, a new custom arose. When a dragon was dying, they could gift their heart stone to another—usually their heir."

"And they can be gifted to humans?" Lainey rubbed her stone again.

"Yes. It started early in our association with your kind."

Renick looked down and pushed a rock around in the sand with his finger. "Louren and his dragon?"

"You know many tales from our past, Renick-Trusted." Derth laughed. "Yes, Louren and Dothar Nathernest."

Renick recognized "nathernest" as the term his father used to identify a hatchling that was rejected by its mother—usually because of a deformity. He had not known the connection to the fable.

"When a dragon stone is gifted to a human," Derth continued, "it gives them access to that magical power."

"So I have magic like you now?" Lainey asked.

"We dragons are limited in the use of our magic. Humans seem to be able to use it in a wider variety of ways." Derth tilted his head. "Someone will need to instruct you on its use."

"We will find someone," Wrytha said. Derth and Wrytha exchanged a look and a message in dragon-speak that was hidden from Renick.

"Very well. Any questions?" Derth turned to Renick and the others.

"Are the stones the reason why humans hunt dragons?" Renick asked.

At the same moment, Thane said, "Derth said we were in danger—why?"

"Renick, yes. But that is a story for another day." Derth turned to Thane. "It has been a long time since a dragon gifted their stone to a human. That, coupled with the uneasiness your presence here has caused and the delicate nature of your position, makes Junther's act a dangerous one."

"He meant well," Lainey said in a hushed voice.

"He did," Wrytha agreed. "But many of our kind will not understand. They will be fearful and wish to destroy you."

"I spoke with Flyn and Junther at length last night. He knew his decision would put you all in danger. My son and I have a way to protect you." Grane looked at each of them in turn.

"Grane." Derth's gravelly voice cut through the other dragon's words. "What are you planning?"

Grane continued without acknowledging Derth. "I wish to adopt the three of you into my clan."

"What?" A jet of flame exploded from Derth's mouth. The heat brushed against Renick's face and he turned away. Plyth let out a surprised yelp.

"Hush!" Wrytha chastised her brother for his outburst with a flick of her tail.

"It is unheard of," Derth grumbled.

"Not entirely," Grane said. "There is dragon law to cover just such a situation. They would be granted all the rights and privileges of the Dragon Kind and be our kin. It will save them."

Derth came to stand face-to-face with Grane, their snouts so close they were almost touching. "But it will not end the turmoil. Many will still not accept them—in fact, many will fear them even more. Junther's decision was a rash one that could cost Lainey her life."

Plyth whined and buried his head in Lainey's lap.

"Shhh, it's all right." She stroked his scales and spoke softly in his ear. No trace of the fear in her face made it to her voice.

"If it puts her in danger, take it out," Thane said.

Wrytha shook her head. "It is not that simple. It is the act of gifting the stone, not her possession of it, which causes the danger. And that cannot be undone."

"We have to do something," Thane pressed. "Maybe we could tell the dragons that Lainey rejected the gift."

"Enough," Boren called. "What is done is done."

"Well said, Boren." Grane turned to Renick. "Renick-Trusted, I invite you to be my kin, to join my clan and to be counted among my own."

"Grane." Derth gave a warning growl.

Grane ignored Derth. "Do you accept, Renick-Trusted?"

Renick's mouth fell open. "I ... I'm honored, but ... but I ..."

"Grane, you are confusing the boy," Wrytha hissed. "Renick-Trusted, if you are made a part of Grane's clan, it would mean that you would be held to all dragon laws, that you would be part of our society and one of our kin. It is a decision that should not be rushed."

"My thoughts exactly," Derth grumbled.

"We do not have time for this." Grane started pacing back and forth.

"Being rash will not help them," Derth started to argue.

"I accept," Renick said firmly.

"Renick," Lainey whispered.

"Are you sure?" Thane asked.

Renick turned to his friends. "We're in danger anyway. And I for one would ..." He could not find the words to express his feelings. He faced the dragons again. "I've never given up hope that my father's stories held some truth. And here I am, standing in the middle of a place built out of the stories. I want to be a part of it, no what matter the danger."

For a long while, everyone was silent.

It was Grane who finally spoke. "Thane-Brave, I make you the same invitation. Do you accept?"

Thane squared his shoulders. "Yes."

"And Lainey-Kind, do you—"

"Yes," Lainey answered before Grane could finish his question.

"There." Grane turned to Derth, a sly look in his eye. "It is done."

"You have always been too proud for your own good. Now we have much to deal with before tomorrow morning."

"What is happening tomorrow morning?" Lainey asked as she nuzzled her nose against Plyth's.

"The council is meeting to decide your fate." Grane sat and watched Derth's agitated movement.

"We need a plan of action. They will be safe here, but one of us should stay with them just in case," Derth said.

"Derth." Grane waited until the dark-blue dragon stopped to look up at him. "I intend to suggest that they," he tilted his head toward Renick, Thane, Lainey and Plyth, "be spoken."

Lainey turned to Renick, a question on her face. "What is being spoken?" she asked in a whisper.

He shrugged and answered in just as quiet a tone. "I don't know."

There was a thump as Derth sat down hard. "Does your audacity know no bounds, Grane? Our society exists in a state of delicate balance—do you plan to topple it altogether?"

Renick whispered to his friends, "Whatever it is, it seems to be important."

Lainey and Thane nodded, and then they all turned back to watch the adult dragons argue.

"Would you choose war or peace?" Grane asked Derth.

This made Derth's mouth fall open. Then his jaws snapped shut. "I have always opposed the war. You know that better than anyone."

Grane nodded. "And I once vehemently disagreed with you. But my stance has changed. We can never attain peace—never stop the war—unless we make a change. Talking is not enough. I am acting to upset the balance so we can realign ourselves to a new way of thinking."

"You are playing a dangerous game with three lives." Smoke curled up from Derth's nostrils.

"Their lives were already in danger."

"I dislike being discussed like this," Thane said just loud

enough for Renick and Lainey to hear.

"Then why don't you speak up?" Lainey rolled her eyes at him.

"Because they are *dragons*, and they breathe *fire*."

Wrytha sighed. "Enough. You both have the same goal in mind—you just go about it in different ways."

"We still need a plan for how to iron out Grane's mess," Derth insisted.

"While you two were squabbling, Wrytha and I have formulated just such a plan," Boren said with a yawn.

"And?" Derth flapped his wings just enough to stir the dirt around him.

"You and Grane must elicit aid in your petition to have the young ones spoken. Boren and I will watch over them while you are gone." Wrytha nodded her head once, as if there would be no further discussion. Grane and Derth looked at each other and then both dipped their heads.

"We will return by nightfall," Derth promised, and he and Grane disappeared into the cave opening.

"What is being spoken?" Lainey asked of Wrytha.

"When a dragon comes of age, his or her name is spoken in the dragon hall. That is when we are placed in the circle to which we belong. It is rite of passage," she explained.

"And humans can be spoken too?" Renick asked. His heart jumped a little at the thought of such a wondrous possibility.

A rush of air came out from between Wrytha's teeth. "Once, yes. Back in the old days when relations between our two kinds were best, there was a special circle—a circle for the humans whom the dragons wished to honor. But that circle has been empty for many generations."

"And Grane feels we have earned such an honor?" Thane's eyes narrowed when Wrytha bobbed her head in confirmation. "That is quite a different view from what he held just a few days ago."

"Thane-Brave," Wrytha turned so she could train one eye on him, "not all dragons are as stubborn as Derth. Some of us have a fluid view of the world. Grane is one of them. He has seen that he was wrong and now stands behind his new beliefs just as adamantly as he did his old."

"Question is," Boren said, "is it enough?"

Wrytha looked after Grane and Derth. "We can only hope."

Marked

Renick shifted his weight to his other foot, which throbbed in protest. At least the dragon hall was growing warmer now that the sun poured light directly down into it. Next to him, Thane stifled a yawn. Derth trained a stern but knowing look on the boy. Plyth let out a little yip of laughter at their exchange, and Wrytha had to wrap her front claws around him to silence him.

"Enough," the gold dragon roared into the chaos around them.

The entire audience gathered in the dragon hall fell quiet.

"The time for debate is over; the facts remain." The gold dragon spread his wings wide and rose to stand on his hind legs. "The dragon-named found our city and returned Plyth Firetongue to us. They rescued two of our own at great peril to themselves, and as a reward, one was gifted a stone and all were accepted into a dragon clan."

Unrest began to trickle through the dragon council again. The gold dragon spewed smoke as a warning.

"We cannot change what is in the past," he continued. "All that remains is to decide. Are there any who wish to speak on behalf of the dragon-named?"

A chorus of dragon bugles filled the hall. Renick turned to

look behind him. Wrytha and Derth both had their heads raised, deep tones coming from their open mouths. He scanned the hall and saw that Boren and Mryx were also lending their voices to the chorus. On the pedestals of the Second Circle, Grane roared too.

The chorus stopped and the sound faded. "Very well, Boren Underwing, speak."

Boren took a few swaying steps forward. "I speak for the dragon-named." What followed was a stream of images and feelings that were so deep and concentrated that Renick's tired mind had problems sorting them out. He thought what Boren was saying went along the lines of, "These three have shown valor and courage. They have done much with great effect on me. I would put my life in their hands without a second thought."

The human words did not seem to do the dragon-speak justice. But Renick could feel Boren's meaning, and the dragon's confidence in him pressed heavily on his heart.

When Boren finished, he spread his wings wide. "I vote they be spoken."

The hall filled with a clatter of flapping wings, trumpets, and growls, but a warning jet of flame from the gold dragon calmed them.

"Mryx Clawmender, speak."

Mryx moved to stand where Boren had been moments before. "I speak on behalf of Junther Swiftwing, who is no longer among us. He votes with Boren. They should be spoken." This was met by an even greater response than Boren's words.

There was an uneasy shifting among many of the dragons in the hall. The gold dragon ignored this and turned to Wrytha. "Speak."

Renick turned to watch her. She dipped her head. "I speak for Plyth Firetongue, whose name has not yet been spoken. He trusts those he named."

Her words struck Renick. Something deep within him stirred and would not settle.

"Derth Wisescales of the Second Circle, speak." The gold dragon's words brought Renick back to the moment at hand.

"There is little I can add to what others have said. I offer only this: Plyth Firetongue's trust is well placed." Derth stepped back. Again, that something in Renick fluttered, its unrest growing.

The last to be called on was Grane. He sat back on his hind legs, stretched his neck and wings out, and then bowed to Renick and his friends. Everything seemed to hang still. No one moved. No one spoke. The breath was locked in Renick's chest and only his heart felt free to move.

In the center of the hall, the gold dragon looked thoughtful. His head was lowered almost to the ground. "Lainey-Kind, do you have anything to say for yourself?"

Lainey looked a little startled. She wrapped her arms around herself and cast a weary glance at Renick. He nodded in support and she stepped forward and dropped her hands. "I'm deeply touched by Junther Swiftwing's gift and vow to use it as he asked—to help and assist others. I'm honored ..." Lainey stood there for a few moments opening and closing her mouth. Eventually she stepped back.

"Thane-Brave?"

Thane strode forward boldly. "All I ask for is freedom." He resumed his position to Renick's right.

"Renick-Trusted, please step forward," the gold dragon said.

Renick's stomach fell. He swallowed hard and took an uncertain step forward. "I ..." he looked around at the dragons in the hall and swallowed again. "I don't know why Plyth named me Trusted. I've always tried to be trustworthy. But I'm not infallible. I ..." He searched for more to say. There was so much in his heart that he could not find the words. Thinking back to the night before, he collected everything he was feeling. He compressed it into a single thought and pushed it toward the center of the hall.

Wings fluttered and dragons shifted. There were a few yelps of surprise around the hall as the dragons reacted to Renick's communication. Unsure how to continue, Renick turned to Derth, who only urged him on. Renick took a moment to collect his thoughts. "For what it's worth," he said, "if you put your trust in me, I'll do my best to never let you down." He turned his back on the gathered dragons, his shoulders slumped and his head down. When he stood once again between Thane and Lainey, he looked up. Derth was watching him.

Renick shrugged and turned to face the Inner Circle once more.

"There is much to be considered." At the gold dragon's word, many of the dragons in the hall started murmuring. Images and emotions jumbled in Renick's head and he was glad to realize it did not hurt. His mind had at last become accustomed to the dragons' form of communication.

"The time for debate is over!" Grane roared into the hall. "I call for a final vote."

"Agreed." The gold dragon waited for all to grow quiet. "Who favors that the dragon-named be spoken?"

Renick was surprised to see that all save a few of the dragons on the council lifted their heads and blew a small jet of hot air into the cavern. The walls seemed to writhe behind the dragons' breath.

"The Inner Circle has decided. The dragon-named will be spoken." There was a conflicting clatter of noise throughout the hall.

"Plyth," the gold dragon said. Wrytha pushed Plyth forward. "I name you in the dragon hall as Plyth Firetongue of the Trusted Circle." As the dragon spoke, a single blue jewel flickered to life on the wall of the hall. An impression formed in the rock, spreading out from the stone and curving back to form a circle. Renick turned and saw an answering light glowing in Plyth's chest.

"Lainey, I name you in the dragon hall as Lainey-Kind of the Trusted Circle, and Trusted of the Dragon Kind." Across from Plyth's jewel, a yellow one formed, its light steady and strong. The heart stone hidden under Lainey's blouse flashed with a renewed light and then faded back to its dim glow.

"Thane, I name you in the dragon hall as Thane-Brave of the Trusted Circle, and Trusted of the Dragon Kind." A red jewel appeared in between Plyth's and Lainey's on the bottom edge of the circle.

"Renick." As the gold dragon spoke, a strange heat pulsed through Renick's body. "I name you in the dragon hall as Renick-Trusted of the Trusted Circle, and Trusted of the Dragon Kind." A green jewel appeared opposite Thane's—it shone brightest of them all. The heat in his chest dissipated, leaving a tingle that lingered for some time.

The gold dragon nodded to Derth, who was seated on his pedestal. Derth rose and addressed Renick and his friends. "Your names have been spoken. You are now counted as kin of the Dragon Kind. The Circle of the Trusted is begun again."

Grane moved forward. "As part of being named, you will also be marked," he said, "so that all dragons will know that you are Trusted." Grane leapt from his pedestal and landed in front of Renick. The dragon turned first to Lainey. He breathed a wave of hot air on her. The breath pushed back her hair and rustled her dress. A yellow light formed a rune in the hollow of Lainey's collarbones. Renick recognized the symbol from the same book where he had seen Horrin's tattoo. He tried, but could not remember what the rune meant.

"Thane-Brave, hold out your right hand," Grane instructed. Thane complied, extending his arm with his right hand in a fist. "Other way." The dragon seemed to smile. Thane flipped his hand over and spread out his fingers. Grane's breath caused a red light to draw another rune on Thane's palm. After the light faded, Thane flexed his hand a few times and the rune vanished. Renick looked over at Lainey—her rune had faded as well.

Finally, Grane turned to Renick. "Remove your ... skin?" the dragon asked.

Renick smiled. Lainey let out a little laugh. "You mean my shirt?" Renick said. The dragon nodded. He peeled the torn garment over his head. Grane blew uncomfortably hot air on his left arm, just below the shoulder. The warmth spread through Renick like it had when he was spoken. A green light, that felt like a finger, gently traced the design of a rune. When the form was complete, the light went out and the rune faded.

He could still feel the mark on him. Renick wondered if the sensation would ever go away as he pulled his shirt back on.

Grane returned to his place in the circle. The gold dragon raised his head. "We are entrusting you with our secret. Keep it safe. "

Renick joined Lainey and Thane in a murmured, "We will." Renick felt the rune on his arm burn and the heat spread through him. He looked down and could see his mark glowing green through the fabric of his shirt.

"It is done," the gold dragon said. He spread his wings and rose slightly in the air.

With an eruption of wingbeats, the dragons departed and the cavern stood mostly empty. Renick scanned the pedestals and found Derth still sitting on his. The dragon glided over to them.

"Come," Derth said and led them down a passageway.

As they walked, Renick was deep in contemplation and finally asked, "Why did the dragons react that way to my thoughts?"

"You used our native tongue instinctively," Derth answered. "No other human has ever done that before. And they were impressed by the depth and intelligence behind your words."

Renick nodded, an odd mix of pride and anxiety spreading through him.

"What about these marks?" Thane asked. "If they've faded, how will other dragons know to trust us?"

"They are magic. The dragons will sense them," Wrytha said.

"Why is Plyth part of the circle?" Lainey asked.

"Each dragon circle must have at least one dragon. Plyth is like the dragon ambassador," Wrytha answered.

"Ambassador!" Plyth squealed, jumped into the air and

used his wings to hover there for a moment.

Wrytha laughed. "Yes, Plyth, it is quite an honor for one as young as you."

"Where're we going?" Thane said.

"We are taking you home," Wrytha answered.

Lainey and Thane exchanged glances, their eyes excited. Renick's heart sank a little. "Home or to Trevinni?"

Wrytha cocked her head. "Where would you like to go?"

Renick could not answer her question. He wished to see his family and home again, but that part of his life was over now. Searching inside, Renick found that his fear of striking out on his own was still there. Even after all they had been through, Renick was unsure of his future.

Lainey's eyebrows scrunched together.

Everyone seemed to be looking to him for an answer. Renick shrugged and turned away. "I want to stay here," he whispered and hoped that no one heard.

"We should go to Trevinni," Thane said. Looking up, Renick saw Thane's eyes on him. With a slight tightening of his lips, he thanked the older boy for his assistance.

Renick turned back to face the others. He stood tall and nodded. "I agree. If anyone is looking for us, that's where they'd expect to find us."

"To Trevinni it is, then," Derth said.

"What about ... this," Lainey asked, tapping her heart stone. "Others will see it."

"By the time we reach the edge of the forest the stone will have completed it works and I will remove it." Wrytha answered.

"Remove it?" Lainey sounded sad.

"You can keep it as token. In the old times humans used to fashion jewelry out of them," Derth offered.

"I like that idea," Lainey smiled to herself as they left the confines of the mountain and emerged into the sunlit forest.

All around them, trees danced in a gentle breeze and the earth smelled wet and new. Lainey took a deep breath and lifted her face to the sky.

"I never would've thought I'd be happy to see the forest again!" She giggled and ran around a few trees before returning to stand with them. "Isn't it a beautiful day?"

Derth shook his head and hummed. "Lainey-Kind, you are a creature of air, and not meant to be confined to caves."

Wrytha dipped her head. "Look how different the girl acts when not enclosed."

Renick smiled. "You have no idea." He rolled his eyes in mock frustration.

Lainey crossed her arms and pouted. "I thought you liked me."

Thane put his arm around her shoulders. "Lainey, you're one of a kind." Together they all laughed.

"How will we get to Trevinni?" Renick asked when the mirth subsided.

Derth spread his wings. "We fly."

I No Longer Fit

The wind whipped past Renick's face and made his nose cold. Below him, the forest was just a blur of green. The sun shone bright in the sky, reflecting off the clouds. Above him, Derth's large form glided protectively, keeping watch for danger. Renick uncoiled his hands from around one of Wrytha's neck spikes and let them hover for a moment. He bobbed up and down to the rhythm of her wings beating. When he had steadied himself, Renick spread his arms out wide.

A thrill of excitement shot through him. Lifting his face to the sky, Renick closed his eyes and absorbed the weightless feeling.

Lainey giggled. Renick turned to watch her. She too had her arms spread out. When Renick caught her eye, she jerked her head behind her. Getting a good grip on Wrytha's neck spike, Renick leaned over so he could see Thane.

Thane sat hunched over Wrytha's tail, a death grip on her spikes. His face was ashen and he looked as if he might lose his breakfast. Renick laughed. Thane looked up at him and glared. He yelled something at Renick, but the wind tore it away.

Wrytha's neck rumbled. "You young ones are so amusing."

Plyth let go of the end of Wrytha's tail and came to glide

next to Renick. He chattered and flapped his wings. "Fly!" Plyth's voice echoed in Renick's ear. "Fly!"

The young dragon fell back again and flew circles around Thane, who did not look at all happy with his antics.

Renick called out to Wrytha, "I think Thane needs a break."

The white dragon arched her neck to look back at Thane. She rumbled again. "Yes. Not all humans are suited to flying, I see. Hold on!" She beat her wings a few times and then dove for the forest. Renick grabbed the spike in front of him just in time. Lainey's shout of glee rose almost to a scream. Thane, on the other hand, *did* scream. It sounded much like Lainey's— except more terrified. Renick could not keep from laughing.

Finding a gap in the trees, Wrytha pulled back and hovered above the ground, her tail laid across the dirt. Thane groaned and rolled off her tail, landing with a thump. He lay staring up at the sky, his face a little green.

Wrytha descended the rest of the way. She lay on the ground and waited while Renick climbed down from her neck and moved to help Lainey off her back.

"Thank you!" Lainey exclaimed breathlessly. "That was the most wonderful experience of my life. To be flying!" She twirled excitedly.

Wrytha's eyes narrowed in amusement. Renick bowed to the dragon and offered his thanks also.

The grass in the small clearing stirred as Derth landed beside them.

"You two are crazy!" Thane moaned. "That was terrible."

"What's wrong?" Renick said, unable to help himself. "Are you afraid of flying on the big scary dragon? Or do you always scream like a girl when landing?"

"Shut up, Renick," Thane grumbled.

Wrytha turned her head so she could see Thane still sprawled on the ground. "Fear not, little one. We are almost close enough to the forest's edge now that flying any further would put us at risk. So we might as well finish our journey with your feet firmly on the ground."

Thane let out a little sob of relief. Lainey knelt beside him and helped him drink from his waterskin.

"There, does that help?" she asked. Thane nodded his head. When he had sufficiently recovered, they set out again—on foot. Derth led the way, weaving a trail through the larger gaps between the trees. When there was not a way that would accommodate him, he simply made one. Wrytha brought up the rear, sweeping her tail along the growth to hide their footprints, although it hardly disguised their trail.

"I wish you two had been with us from the start. You would've saved us a lot of trouble," Thane said.

"The only way to travel," Derth answered, "is with a dragon." They all laughed together.

Just as the sun started to sink toward its final descent of the day, they stopped.

"Those trees ahead mark the edge of the forest," Wrytha told them. "If you keep walking, you will find the road to your village."

Renick stared at the line of trees and the open fields of grass beyond. His heart pounded in his chest and his palms turned cold with sweat. He did not want to go. Renick felt like leaving the forest would be like waking from a dream. He did not want to let it go.

"Lainey, come here." Wrytha bent her head low.

Lainey complied, stepping closer to Wrytha. The white dragon placed her nose on Lainey's chest and hummed. The heart stone slipped free and fell to the ground. Lainey scooped it up and cradled it in her hands for a few moments before stowing it safely in her healers pouch.

"Be careful of your magic, young one. Do not let others know you posses it," Wrytha offered in warning. Lainey raised her fist to her heart and bowed slightly to Wrytha in acknowledgement.

Plyth whined sadly. "Time for good-bye?"

"Just good-bye for now, Plyth. You and I are staying here to watch over and teach your friends," Wrytha said. She turned to face Renick, Thane, and Lainey. "We will find a safe place to live, and then I will call for you."

Lainey turned her face up to Wrytha. "Thank you." She knelt beside Plyth and wrapped her arms around him. "Goodbye, Plyth. You be careful out here." She turned and offered Derth a parting smile.

Thane patted Plyth on the head and mumbled something. He also bid farewell to Wrytha and Derth.

Renick did not know what to do. Partings were always awkward for him. Not knowing what to say, he simply rubbed Plyth's nose and waved to Wrytha and Derth.

Together he, Thane, and Lainey turned to leave the woods.

"Farewell, my friends." Derth dipped his head.

"Farewell, Trusted of the Dragon Kind," Wrytha said as she, Derth, and Plyth melted back into the forest.

Lainey took Renick's hand. He turned to see her smiling at him. She took Thane's hand as well and the three of them started walking, slowly at first and then more quickly as they gained confidence. Before long, they emerged from the forest into the fading light of sunset.

Renick stopped, releasing Lainey's hand.

"What is it?" she asked.

"It feels," he shrugged, "different."

Thane nodded. "I know what you mean. Like the world's changed and we no longer quite fit."

Lainey shook her head. "It's not the world that's changed—it's us. Our perception has been altered by what we've learned. We may never fit anywhere again."

Renick thought about that for a time. "I don't mind." He looked at the others. "The not fitting."

Thane smiled. "I never really fit before."

Lainey thought that was amusing, Renick could see the laugh in her eyes—even though she did not voice it.

"Come on," she said. "I want a hot meal, a warm bath, and a soft bed tonight." She linked arms with Renick and Thane and pulled them forward once again.

Renick looked up to the sky, the day was coming to an end, and the air had a slight chill to it.

"Do you think the others will be waiting for us?" Lainey

asked.

Thane picked a rock up from the road and threw it ahead of them. It bounced several times before disappearing into the long grass. "I was wondering if they even survived."

"I bet they're okay," Renick said. He was not entirely sure he believed that, but it seemed to be what Lainey needed to hear. She smiled at him softly.

"I'm sure your parents are sick with worry. They're probably watching the road as we speak, hoping to see you," Lainey offered.

Renick's shoulders slumped. "There's too much for them to do. I doubt they travelled all the way out here. It's a critical time in the breeding season—my father could never slip away. And my mother has the little ones to tend." He tried to sound nonchalant, like he was okay with being just one in a crowd.

Lainey put a hand on his arm. "I'm sure someone's waiting for you."

The roof of a tall building cut into the horizon. "Look." Renick pointed. They moved closer and more buildings came into view. Some already had candles burning in their windows. "What do we do when we—"

Lainey was cut off by a shout. Renick turned to see four figures racing towards them from the edge of town. Renick stopped, stunned. Thane's hand went to his sword.

"Aunt Melatheen!" Lainey shrieked and started running. A short way off, she fell into her aunt's arms, sobbing.

Thane jogged to meet up with Grahm. They greeted each other with a brisk handshake and concealed smiles.

Renick almost lost his balance when he recognized the two other people—two of his older brothers, Greyson and Penter. He ran to stand beside them. "What're you doing here?" he exclaimed. He danced on his toes, wanting to hug his brothers but afraid they would think it childish.

Penter, his oldest brother, bent down and lifted Renick in a big bear hug. "Renick! We came to find you." When Penter released him, Renick saw that tears were shining in his brother's eyes. Penter never cried. Never.

"Mother's been beside herself with worry. She took to bed after hearing the news of your disappearance. Father would've come himself, but he dared not leave her side," the always calm Greyson explained.

Penter slapped Renick on the back. "Don't ever do that to us again, you hear?"

Renick laughed. "I won't." His brothers engulfed him in another hug. Renick looked over and saw Lainey smiling at him as she chatted with her aunt. They all gathered together and everyone was introduced.

"Nice to meet everyone and all, but I'm cold, and hungry, and tired." Lainey punctuated her words with a yawn.

"Come." Melatheen wrapped her arm around her niece.

As they walked into town, Melatheen and Grahm explained what happened to them after the crash. They were thrown far from the passenger basket. They found the wreckage of the flyer two days after the crash. When the children were not to be found, they decided it would be best to head for Trevinni to get help.

"You weren't hurt?" Lainey asked.

"Not badly enough to test Melatheen's skill," Grahm said with a wink.

Melatheen waved off his praise. "We were all right."

"Your brothers arrived only a day after we did," Grahm continued.

Grayson nodded. "We tried to organize a search party right away, but the flyer operators insisted on doing a fly-over first. They didn't even declare the flyer missing until yesterday."

Penter growled and balled his hands into fists. "Darn mud-eating ..." Grayson laid a hand on Penter's shoulder and looked pointedly at Lainey and Melatheen. Penter coughed. "...men."

"They had you as witnesses to the crash and that wasn't enough?" Thane asked.

"Politics, my boy, politics," Grahm said with a shake of his head.

"Well, we're safe now," Lainey said. Her face beamed.

"What about you?" Melatheen asked. "What happened to

you?"

Thane, Lainey, and Renick exchanged glances. "Oh, not much," Lainey answered. A smile tugged at the corners of her mouth.

"There were the wolves," Thane commented.

"And the waterfall," Renick added.

"Oh, and I almost drowned!" Lainey said. At Melatheen's horrified look, she added quickly, "Thane saved me."

"Sounds like an awful lot happened to you three," Penter said.

Renick smiled to himself. "You could say that."

Epilogue

Renick sat on the floor of the stall, the sick dragon's head in his lap. He gently rubbed the soft scales under her chin. Her breath pulled in and out, rasping across her dry throat. Renick's uncle Loren handed him a waterskin. He put its tip between the teeth at the opening of the dragon's jaw and squeezed.

The dragon tossed her head weakly. The water splashed onto Renick's lap and the hay that covered the floor. Renick put the waterskin down and began stroking her chin again.

"It doesn't look good, does it?" Renick asked.

His uncle's brow furrowed and he placed a hand on Renick's shoulder. "Melatheen will be here soon. She'll know what to do."

Renick nodded, but he did not feel much confidence. The dragon—May was her name—had taken to Renick right away when he started his apprenticeship. In a few short months they had formed a tight bond. And now she lay in his lap, dying. Renick's eyes started to burn and he blinked rapidly to stave off the tears.

"Loren?" a voice called from the stable entrance.

Renick's uncle stood. "Over here, Melatheen."

Footsteps approached and then Lainey's aunt came into view, her stern face more solemn than usual. "Hello, Renick," she said.

The stall door opened and Melatheen entered. Lainey strolled in behind her. Her eyes were narrowed and the corner of her mouth pulled downward. "Are you okay?" Lainey asked as she knelt beside Renick.

"May's the one that's sick." Renick's voice came out sounding rough and hoarse. He coughed to clear it.

Lainey patted his shoulder. "It'll be okay."

Renick watched Melatheen as she examined the sick dragon. The longer she worked, the deeper the frown on her face became. After what felt like days, she sat back and wiped the sweat from her forehead with the back of her sleeve.

"Well?" Uncle Loren asked.

"I just don't know," Melatheen admitted. "It could be any number of things, each with a different course of treatment."

"Can you make a guess?" Uncle Loren's hands tightened into fists. May belonged to a very rich client who happened to be away at the moment. If they lost her, it would not only devastate Renick, but ruin his uncle's reputation.

Melatheen shook her head. "I dare not risk making things worse. Stay with her tonight; see if you can get her to drink. I'll come back in the morning. Maybe time will aid us."

Uncle Loren nodded his head. "Renick, you stay here with May tonight. I'll send out blankets, food, and water. Come get me if there's any change."

Renick nodded and returned his attention to May. Uncle Loren and Melatheen stood. "Thank you for coming, Melatheen."

"Any time, Loren." Together, the two of them turned to leave. "Lainey," Melatheen called from the stable entrance.

"Coming! Just a moment," Lainey responded. Renick looked up at her. "I'd offer to use healing magic, but ..."

Renick shrugged. "I know—others might see."

"If only my magic were as discreet as Wrytha's." She smiled at him.

"I wish I could talk to May," Renick lamented.

Lainey's eyes turned soft and sad. "You know you can't. Remember what Derth said?"

Renick shook his head. "I know. But I look in her eyes—all of their eyes—and I have to believe that somewhere inside they have the capacity. That they can talk."

"Hoping for the impossible won't make it so."

Renick turned away from her and hugged May's head closer to him.

After a moment of silence, Lainey slipped away.

Alone with May, Renick let himself feel the growing sorrow and fear. "If only you could speak," he whispered to May. "Then perhaps you could tell me what's wrong." Then, on a whim, he reached out to her like he did with Plyth. He searched for her voice, calling to her.

Pain.

A cold chill ran down Renick's back. The touch felt familiar, but not like it was from May. It was more sinister. The image of a black dragon surrounded by stone surfaced from his memory. "The mines," he whispered to himself.

I will avenge her.

There was an explosion and a chorus of screams pierced the night.

The End

About the Author

Krista Wayment has been making up stories since she learned to talk. Writing naturally grew out of that. Krista is an avid Fantasy and Science Fiction fan, and a total nerd. She is also a software engineer and loves playing video games. Although, curling up with a good book is still one of her favorite past times.

www.kristawayment.com
www.dragonstrust.com

Acknowledgements

It takes a village to write a book. I would like to thank my village for helping to bring this one to life. First and foremost, my mother who fostered and encourage my love of writing from a young age. And who loved this story from the first moment I told her about the idea.

Next I must thank those who helped to shape this story into what it is today, starting from the beginning. Thanks to Laura D. Bastian, Melanie Skelton, and Holli Anderson for listening to my idea on the way back from the LDS Storymakers conference. A tip of the hat to my Alpha Readers: Krista McLaughlin, Christina Cook, and Terron James. Thanks for helping me to hash out so many details. And speaking of hashing out details, thanks to Lauren Ritz, Heidi Tighe, Anya Kimlin, Terrie Lynn Bittner, Gussie Fick, Laura Josephsen, and all my other iWriteNetwork friends. Also a shout out to my Facebook friends for coming to the rescue with important details and personal experiences that helped give this story that little something extra. Much thanks to my Beta Readers: Nanette O'Neal, Donea Weaver, and Meredith Mansfield for all your wonderful comments and suggestions. I must also mention my fellow Pied Piper critique group members who helped me improve my writing skills. And finally to my editors, Tristi Pinkston and her assistant Maria, for whipping this manuscript into shape.

A final acknowledgment to you—the reader. We did this for you. I hope you enjoyed the story.

Made in the USA
Middletown, DE
29 June 2019